THE SHADOW WEAVER

Dear Reader,

Thank you so much for picking up a copy of my first book. Your support means the world to me and has helped me take the first step on this exciting journey as a new author.

I hope you enjoy the story and that it brings a bit of magic into your day.

Warm regards,

David J Mumford

THE SHADOW WEAVER

DAVID J MUMFORD

Contents

1

I. Friction

The rain had been falling steadily since morning, drumming softly against the window of Po's small room. He liked it when it rained—it made Portadale even quieter than usual. From his window, Po could see the still, familiar rows of red-brick houses and narrow streets, winding their way through the quiet suburban town. The rain-soaked rooftops and empty streets made him feel safe. Portadale wasn't exciting, but at least it was predictable.

"Come on, Po," Zap said, his imaginary tail wagging as he bounced beside the bed. "Let's go outside. It's just a bit of rain! No one else will be out there."

Po shook his head. "No. Not today. Besides, it's not just the rain," he muttered. "It's what's out there." He glanced toward the edge of town where the houses stopped, and the world beyond began.

Zap cocked his head, his grin widening. "What do you mean, *out there*? You're not still scared of what's outside Portadale, are you?"

Po sighed. "It's not just that. It's... different. Unpredictable. There are bigger towns, more people, and anything could happen. Here, everything's just... the same." He trailed off, his eyes fixed on the familiar rooftops of Portadale. Out there, beyond the town's quiet streets, was a world full of the unknown—and that was exactly what made Po anxious.

Zap's eyes twinkled mischievously. "But different can be good, Po! Who knows, maybe you'll discover something incredible. Don't you want to explore?" He tilted his head as if he knew something Po didn't, a flicker of mystery in his playful gaze.

Po thought about it for a moment. Adventure always sounded exciting when Zap talked about it, but in Po's mind, it just meant a lot of unexpected, uncontrollable things.

Just then, his mum's voice called from downstairs. "Po, time for school!"

Po snapped out of his thoughts. School. Another place full of unpredictable moments. He felt a tight knot form in his stomach. He grabbed his school bag, gave Zap a nod, and headed out the door.

The rain had lightened by the time Po reached Portadale Secondary School. It was still drizzling, but the steady rhythm of his shoes splashing through puddles calmed him a little. The familiar brick building loomed ahead, with only a few students trudging through the schoolyard.

As Po slipped into his seat in Mrs. Yin's science class, he relaxed a bit. Science always made sense to him. It was the one subject where everything had a reason, a rule, or a formula to follow. There was no guessing, no hidden meaning. Just facts.

Mrs. Yin, a petite woman with sharp eyes and a kind smile, stood at the front of the room, adjusting her white lab coat. She clapped her hands for attention. "Alright, class, today we're going to talk about *friction*," she began, her voice clear and confident. "It's one of the most important forces in the world. Can anyone tell me what it does?"

Po's hand shot up. "Friction is the resistance that one surface or object encounters when moving over another."

"Exactly!" Mrs. Yin smiled warmly at him. "Friction is all around us, even when we don't realize it. It stops us from slipping when we walk, and it's why things eventually slow down when we push them. But what happens when we reduce friction?"

Po's mind began to race. "If you removed all friction... would things keep moving forever?"

The class fell silent. A few kids snickered under their breath. Po shrank a little in his seat, but Mrs. Yin's smile grew wider.

"That's a fantastic question, Po! In space, without air resistance or friction, objects can move for very long distances. Here on Earth, though, friction is hard to eliminate entirely. However," she added, pacing slightly, "why don't we explore this idea for your next assignment? I want each of you to think about how friction affects your daily lives. What would happen if we didn't have it?"

Groans echoed around the room. Po could feel the glares from the back of the classroom. Damian and Zale—the notorious pair who made everyone's life harder—were already frowning at him. Damian's sharp eyes narrowed, and Zale's lips twisted into a smirk.

"Great, Po. More homework 'cause of you," Damian muttered under his breath as the bell rang, dismissing the class.

Zale leaned in, his voice low and threatening. "Yeah. Just keep your weird mouth shut next time." As Po walked past him, Zale spat on the floor near his shoes, laughing.

Po's stomach churned, but he said nothing. He had learned the hard way that responding only made things worse. He ducked his head, hoisted his backpack onto his shoulder, and slipped out the door as quickly as possible.

Po made his way toward the library. He liked the library—it was quiet, predictable, and filled with books that offered answers.

Right now, he wanted to get a head start on his science assignment, but mostly, he just wanted to avoid the noisy, crowded playground.

The thought of the playground—where kids shouted and laughed and ran around in endless, unpredictable

directions—made Po feel anxious. The library was safe. Quiet. He could already picture himself sitting in his usual corner, surrounded by the smell of old books and the soft sound of pages turning.

But just as he reached the library's double doors, a voice called out from behind him. "Po, wait up!"

Po froze and turned to see Mr. Still, a tall, broad-shouldered teacher with a booming voice, striding towards him. Mr. Still taught PE and was always talking about how kids needed more fresh air and exercise. He also had a way of catching Po at the worst possible moments.

"You're not going in there during break, are you?" Mr. Still asked, eyeing the library doors.

Po shifted nervously. "I was just going to—"

"Get outside, lad! It's break time. You should be out there getting some fresh air, not hiding away in here," Mr. Still said, clapping a firm hand on Po's shoulder and gently steering him towards the door that led to the playground.

Po's heart sank. "But, sir, I—"

"No *buts*, Po. It's important to get outside and move about. You can work on your assignment later." Mr. Still smiled, clearly believing he was doing Po a favour. With a firm pat on the back, he sent Po out into the drizzling playground.

The playground was buzzing with noise—laughter, shouts, the thud of footballs hitting the ground. Po stood on the edge of the chaos, feeling completely out of place. He had nowhere to go, and the noise only made the tightness in his chest grow.

Just as he was about to retreat to the far side of the playground, a voice rang out. "Oi! Po!"

His heart sank. He turned to see Damian and Zale weaving through the crowd toward him. Damian's sharp eyes were locked on him, and Zale followed closely behind, cracking his knuckles and grinning darkly.

"There you are," Damian said as he approached. "We've been looking for you."

Po felt his stomach twist. He took a step back, his mind racing. "I didn't mean—"

"You didn't mean to get us more homework?" Damian interrupted, his voice dripping with sarcasm. "Well, you did. And now you owe us."

Po swallowed hard. "I—I wasn't trying to—"

"Shut it!" Zale growled, stepping up beside Damian. His large frame towered over Po, and his sneer sent a chill down Po's spine. "You always think you're smarter than everyone else."

Before Po could react, Zale spat directly at his face. The warm spit landed on Po's cheek, and he froze, his heart pounding in his chest. A few nearby kids glanced over, but no one intervened. No one ever did.

Po wiped his face quickly, trying to hide the tears that were forming in his eyes. He wanted to say something, but his throat felt tight, like the words were stuck.

"Maybe we should teach you a lesson," Damian said, his voice low and threatening.

Without thinking, Po turned and ran.

He didn't look back—he just ran as fast as his legs would carry him, dodging past kids and sprinting toward the school gates. His heart pounded in his chest, and his breath came in short, panicked bursts. He could hear the footsteps of Damian and Zale thundering behind him, their laughter ringing in his ears.

Out of the school, down the narrow streets of Portadale, Po ran. He didn't know where he was going—he just had to get away. But no matter how fast he ran, he couldn't shake them. His legs burned, his chest ached, and his vision started to blur from the tears he was holding back.

He turned a corner, hoping to lose them, but Damian's voice echoed behind him. "You can't run forever, Po!"

Po's heart sank. He was running out of energy, and they were still right behind him. He glanced around desperately. Up ahead, he spotted something—a small path leading toward a dense forest on the edge of the neighbouring town. The trees looked thick and dark, but Po had no other choice. He darted toward the path, hoping the trees would hide him.

The moment he entered the forest, the air seemed to change. The sounds of the town faded, replaced by the rustling of leaves and the distant chirping of birds. Po weaved between the trees, his breath ragged and his legs trembling from exhaustion. He couldn't hear Damian or Zale anymore, but he didn't stop running.

The forest was darker than he expected, the tall trees blocking out most of the light. His footsteps crunched over the fallen leaves and twigs, and he felt his pulse pounding in his ears. He kept moving, deeper into the forest, until finally, his legs gave out, and he collapsed against a large tree.

"I—I think... I lost them," Po gasped, his chest heaving as he tried to catch his breath.

Zap appeared beside him, his tail wagging. "That was close, Po. I think you're safe for now."

Po nodded, wiping the sweat from his forehead. But as he looked around, he realized he had no idea where he was. The trees stretched endlessly in every direction, and everything looked the same. He was lost.

"I don't know how to get back," Po whispered.

Zap nudged him with his nose. "Maybe it's time to stop running and start looking around."

Po frowned, confused. "For what?"

Zap didn't answer. Instead, he wagged his tail and turned his head toward something in the distance.

Po followed his gaze—and then he saw it.

Just beyond the trees, there was something shimmering. At first, it looked like a patch of mist, but as Po squinted, he realized it was more than that. It was glowing faintly, a swirling mix of colours—blue, green, purple, and gold. The colours shifted and danced, like liquid light hanging in the air.

Po's heart raced again, but this time it wasn't out of fear. It was something else. Curiosity. Wonder.

"What is that?" Po whispered, taking a cautious step toward the glowing mirror.

Zap's tail wagged faster. "Looks like an adventure to me. Or maybe... something more."

Po hesitated, glancing back at the path he'd come from. He could still hear the faint echoes of Damian and Zale's voices in the distance, and the thought of facing them again made his stomach churn. But this... this glowing thing... it felt different. It felt like it was calling him.

Po swallowed hard, then took a deep breath. "Should we... go through it?"

Zap wagged his tail excitedly, his eyes sparkling. "Of course! There might be sausages in there!"

Po couldn't help but crack a small smile. "Sausages, huh? I... guess I am kind of hungry."

Po's heart pounded in his chest as he reached out his hand toward the swirling centre of the mirror. His fingers brushed against the shimmering light, and a wave of calmness spread through him, soothing the anxiety that had been gnawing at him all day.

It didn't feel strange or frightening. Instead, it felt... familiar. Like he'd known this place all along.

Po stepped through the mirror, the shimmering light enveloping him as the world around him shifted. For a moment, everything was soft and blurred, like he was floating in a dream. Then, as quickly as it had begun, the light faded, and Po found himself standing in the middle of something entirely new.

He blinked, his breath catching in his throat. Before him stretched a landscape more beautiful than anything he had ever imagined. The grass beneath his feet was soft and lush, greener than any grass he'd ever seen. Towering trees surrounded him, their leaves shimmering with vibrant emerald hues. Brightly coloured flowers dotted the ground, their petals glowing with shades of pink, orange, and violet, and some of them seemed to sway gently as if they had a life of their own.

Above him, the sky was a brilliant, cloudless blue, the kind that seemed endless and full of possibility. Majestic birds with long, feathered tails soared across the sky, their wings casting shimmering shadows on the ground. They made graceful loops and spirals, as if putting on a show just for him.

In the distance, beyond the rolling hills, something sparkled—a castle. Its towers gleamed in the sunlight, reflecting colours that shifted and danced like rainbows. Po couldn't quite tell what it was made of, but it looked almost like crystal or maybe opal. Whatever it was, it shimmered with an ethereal beauty that left Po breathless.

"Woah..." Po whispered, his eyes wide with wonder. "I wonder what that place is?"

He could hardly believe what he was seeing. A place like this couldn't possibly exist in the real world—it was too perfect, too magical.

Zap trotted up beside him, tail wagging. "Looks like we've got ourselves an adventure!"

Po grinned. For the first time in a long while, the anxiety that had followed him everywhere seemed to fade. He felt... different here. Lighter, braver, like this world was a place where anything was possible.

"Yeah," Po said softly, still staring at the distant castle. "An adventure..."

He turned to look at Zap, ready to share the excitement, but the words caught in his throat.

Zap wasn't the scruffy, imaginary dog he had always known.

He was real.

Po blinked in surprise, his heart skipping a beat. Zap now stood before him as a sleek, golden-furred Shiba Inu, his ears perked up and his dark eyes sparkling with mischief. His fur glistened under the bright sun, and when he barked, it wasn't the soft, imaginary bark Po had always heard in his mind—it was sharp and clear, ringing through the air like music.

"Zap?" Po asked, barely believing his eyes.

Zap looked up at him, his tongue hanging out in a joyful grin. "What do you think? Not bad, huh?"

Po laughed, a sound that felt almost foreign to him. But it was real. Everything here was real. The adventure had begun, and for the first time in a long while, Po wasn't afraid.

As Po gazed out at the vast, magical world before him, a thrill of excitement rushed through him. There was no telling what lay ahead—mysteries, dangers, wonders—but for the first time, that thought didn't scare him. It excited him.

II. Free Candy

Po and Zap walked quietly along the forest path, surrounded by towering trees that seemed to shimmer in the dappled sunlight. The world they had stepped into was unlike anything Po had ever seen, but he couldn't help but feel a lingering unease, even in the beauty of it all.

The trees rustled gently in the breeze, their leaves a vibrant emerald green, and beneath their feet, the soft ground was covered in moss and wildflowers that bloomed in every imaginable colour. The air was crisp and fresh, carrying the scent of earth and flowers. But as Po's gaze lingered on the path, he couldn't shake a gnawing worry—the forest seemed strangely still, almost holding its breath, as if aware of the danger lurking somewhere just beyond their sight.

Zap bounded ahead, his golden fur shining in the sunlight, but he noticed Po's silence and slowed to walk beside him.

"You've been awfully quiet," Zap said, glancing up at Po with a curious look. "Still thinking about Damian and Zale?"

Po frowned; his gaze fixed on the path ahead. "Yeah... I can't stop thinking about them. They always know how to make me feel small. No matter what I do, it's like I can't escape it."

Zap trotted closer, nudging Po gently. "Why do you let them get to you, Po? You're smarter than they are. You just need to stand up to them."

Po sighed. "It's not that easy. I mean, I've tried to ignore them, but they always find a way to make me feel... different. Like I don't belong."

Zap tilted his head thoughtfully. "You know, sometimes standing up for yourself isn't about fighting back. It's about not letting them control how you feel. You've got to stop believing the things they say. You see the world differently, and that's what makes you special."

Po's expression softened, but uncertainty still lingered in his eyes. "Maybe you're right... I just don't know how."

Zap grinned. "You'll figure it out. I'm here to help you with that, too. After all, you've already taken a huge step by coming here. Who knows? Maybe this place will teach you how to handle Damian and Zale when we get back."

Po looked down at Zap, a small smile playing on his lips. "I hope you're right."

"I'm always right," Zap said confidently, his tail wagging. "Now, let's keep going. This forest is way too nice to waste time worrying."

As they walked further, the forest became denser, and the path narrowed. Birds with shimmering feathers flitted between the trees, their songs echoing softly in the distance. The air was cool and refreshing, but Po couldn't shake the feeling that something strange was waiting for them.

Then, up ahead, Po spotted something that made him stop in his tracks. There, nailed to a tree, was a small, weathered sign. The letters were handwritten in dark ink, and as Po squinted, he could just make out what it said.

"Free Candy"

Zap's ears perked up, and his eyes lit up with excitement. "Free candy? This place just keeps getting better and better!" he barked, already bounding toward the sign.

Po raised an eyebrow, confused but intrigued. "Free candy? Why would they just give out candy in the middle of the forest?"

Zap, unfazed, wagged his tail furiously. "Who cares why? We're in a magical place. Maybe it's just how things work around here!"

Po frowned, glancing down the narrow path that led away from the sign. "It feels a little weird to me. But... I guess it wouldn't hurt to check it out."

Zap was already heading down the trail, his enthusiasm bubbling over. "Come on, Po! Candy doesn't just hand itself out every day!"

Reluctantly, Po followed, his curiosity piqued. The path twisted and turned, leading them deeper into the forest. The trees grew taller, their branches weaving together above them to form a canopy that blocked out most of the light. The further they went, the darker and quieter the forest became, until all they could hear was the soft rustling of leaves underfoot. The stillness felt eerie, as though they were being watched.

Eventually, the path opened into a clearing, and Po and Zap came to a stop. Before them was a small village, unlike anything Po had expected. The houses were made of wood and stone, with moss and vines growing over their rooftops. In the centre of the village was a large square, filled with little yellow creatures that bustled about, going about their day with wide smiles on their faces.

The creatures were no taller than Po's waist, with large, round eyes and leaf-like hair that covered their heads and backs. They looked friendly, and as Po and Zap approached, many of them turned to wave and greet them.

"Wow..." Po whispered, taking in the sight of the lively village. "I've never seen anything like this."

Zap trotted beside him, his tail wagging. "I like this place already. These guys look fun!"

As they entered the village, one of the creatures approached them, his eyes wide with excitement. He had a cheerful grin and seemed eager to meet them.

"Welcome, welcome!" the creature said in a bright, friendly voice. "My name is Habzar. Who might you be?"

"I'm Po, and this is Zap," Po replied, glancing around at the other creatures. "We saw the sign that said 'Free Candy'..."

Habzar blinked in confusion for a moment, then laughed. "Ah, I see! You must be new here. The sign... well, it's not quite what you think," Habzar said, chuckling softly. "The sign isn't offering sweets, I'm afraid. It's more of our way of calling for help."

Po blinked, feeling a bit foolish. "Wait, a call for help? But it said..."

"Free Candy, yes." Habzar nodded with a smile. "But it's not about treats. Princess Candy is our beloved ruler, and she has been taken by the Shadow Twins—two terrible beings who have thrown our kingdom into chaos. The sign is our plea for someone brave enough to free her from their grasp."

Zap's ears drooped, clearly disappointed there was no actual candy involved. "No candy, huh?" he muttered. "Bummer."

Po, however, felt his heart start to race again. "Princess Candy? Who are the Shadow Twins? Why did they take her?"

Habzar's expression grew more serious. "The Shadow Twins are creatures of dark magic. They appeared out of nowhere and quickly took control of the lands beyond our village. They kidnapped Princess Candy and locked her away in a hidden fortress. Without her, our kingdom is falling apart—nature is losing its balance, and fear spreads across the land. The sign is our cry for help... for heroes willing to save her."

A few villagers standing nearby nodded solemnly, their faces shadowed with worry. One of them muttered, "Many have tried and failed, but maybe—just maybe—Po and Zap are the ones."

Po's stomach churned. The story reminded him too much of Damian and Zale, the bullies who had terrorized him for so long. The idea of facing another set of cruel beings, even in a magical world, filled him with dread. But something else stirred inside him too—an unexpected sense of duty.

Zap, ever the optimist, brightened up. "A princess in trouble? Sounds like a perfect adventure to me! Let's rescue her, Po!"

Po hesitated, glancing at the villagers' hopeful faces. "I... I don't know. That sounds dangerous."

Habzar stepped forward, his large eyes wide with hope. "We understand if you're scared. The Shadow Twins are no small foes, and they have powers that can make even the bravest warrior quiver. But you two seem strong, and we don't have anyone else to turn to. The villagers would be forever grateful if you helped us."

Po looked at Zap, who was already bouncing with excitement. But he also noticed a flicker of nervousness in Zap's eyes.

"Do you... think we're ready, Zap?" Po asked, his voice hesitant.

Zap paused, his usual confidence wavering for just a moment. "Ready? Who knows. But we've come this far, Po. I'm scared too—those Shadow Twins sound pretty bad—but we can't just ignore people who need us."

Po swallowed hard. The idea of going up against beings as powerful as the Shadow Twins terrified him, but Zap's enthusiasm was infectious. And deep down, Po knew that he couldn't keep running from challenges—not in this world, and not in his own.

He took a deep breath and nodded. "Okay... we'll help. We'll rescue Princess Candy."

Habzar beamed, his wide eyes glowing with excitement. "You don't know how much this means to us, Po and Zap! The village has been waiting for someone brave enough to take on this quest. We'll make sure you're well prepared. But first, we must celebrate your courage!"

"Celebrate?" Po asked, a bit taken aback.

"Oh, yes!" Habzar grinned, clapping his hands together. "A feast in your honour! It's our tradition to hold a grand feast for those who take on a noble quest. It's our way of offering support and showing our gratitude."

Zap's ears perked up, tail wagging furiously. "Did you say 'feast'? Well, that sounds more like it!"

Po hesitated. He had never been one for large gatherings, usually preferring the comfort of quiet spaces, but something about the warmth of the villagers and the thought of their support eased his nerves a little. He looked at Zap, whose excitement was contagious and gave a small nod. "Alright... a feast sounds nice."

Habzar gestured for them to follow. "Come, follow me to the village square. That's where we gather for celebrations."

As they walked, Po took in the details of the village. Small stone cottages with wooden roofs dotted the landscape, some covered in vines and moss, while others had tiny, blooming gardens out front. Yellow lanterns hung from the trees above, casting a soft golden glow over the village even though it was still daylight. Everywhere Po looked, the little yellow villagers were smiling and laughing, their leaf-like hair bouncing as they waved in greeting.

They followed Habzar down a narrow, winding path until they reached the village square, which was nestled beneath the canopy of tall, leafy trees. The centre of the square was already bustling with activity. Long wooden tables were being set up, and the air was filled with the smell of freshly baked bread, roasted vegetables, and sweet pastries. Villagers were placing large bowls of colourful fruits and steaming platters of food along the tables, while others busily strung up more yellow lanterns, giving the square a festive glow.

Zap's eyes widened, and he licked his lips. "This is more like it! I'm starving already!"

Po smiled softly, feeling a little less anxious now that he saw the joy and excitement in the air. The villagers gathered around the square, their big eyes gleaming as they watched him and Zap with admiration and curiosity.

Habzar led Po and Zap to the head of the main table, where two large chairs had been set up just for them. "Please, sit! Tonight, we celebrate new friends and new beginnings."

Po sat down cautiously, feeling the gazes of the villagers on him. For a moment, he felt his usual nervousness creeping in, but then Zap leaped onto his chair, barking cheerfully, "Let's dig in!"

The villagers cheered as plates of food were passed around. Po stared at the feast before him, feeling a bit overwhelmed by the sheer variety—there were roasted fruits that sparkled with golden juices, rich stews bubbling in large clay pots, and pastries piled high with berries that gleamed like jewels.

As they began to eat, the atmosphere grew livelier. Music started up—soft, lilting tunes played by some of the villagers on flutes and small drums. Laughter echoed through the square as the villagers danced and clapped, their energy infectious.

Zap, true to form, was devouring everything within reach. "This is the best feast ever!" he declared between bites of roasted meat. "We should go on quests more often if this is how we're treated!"

Po couldn't help but chuckle. He was starting to feel more comfortable, the warmth of the feast and the laughter of the villagers calming his nerves. For the first time in a long while, he didn't feel out of place. There was no judgment here—just acceptance and encouragement.

Halfway through the feast, Habzar stood up from his seat and tapped on his glass, signalling for quiet. The music faded, and all eyes turned toward him.

"Po and Zap," Habzar began, his voice warm and full of admiration. "Tonight, we celebrate your bravery, and we are grateful that you have agreed to take on the quest to save our beloved Princess Candy. But before you leave, we have a small gift for you."

Habzar motioned for one of the other villagers, who hurried over carrying a small, wooden box. With a smile, Habzar lifted the lid and pulled out a delicate wooden flute, strung on a simple leather cord. The flute was beautifully carved, with intricate patterns running along its sides.

"This," Habzar said, handing the flute to Po, "is a special gift from our village. It may not look like much, but it holds great power. If ever you find yourselves lost or unsure of where to go next, simply play the flute. It will reveal the path—but only when the time is right."

Po held the flute in his hands, running his fingers over the smooth, polished wood. It felt light but sturdy, and there was something comforting about it. He slipped the cord around his neck, the flute resting softly against his chest. "Thank you," Po said, his voice filled with genuine gratitude. "I don't know what to say."

"You've already said enough by agreeing to help us," Habzar replied, smiling warmly. "We believe in you."

Zap, his mouth full of pie, gave an enthusiastic nod. "This is awesome! A magical flute? We're totally set for this adventure now!"

The villagers cheered again, clapping and raising their glasses in a final toast to Po and Zap.

As the evening grew late and the feast began to wind down, Po found himself feeling something unexpected—hope. He glanced at Zap, who was now contentedly lying on his back, too full to move, and smiled. Maybe this quest wasn't as impossible as it first seemed.

With the flute around his neck and the villagers' faith in him, Po felt a new sense of purpose. Tomorrow, they would set off on their journey to rescue Princess Candy, and though he was still nervous, something inside him had shifted. He wasn't just a scared boy anymore—he was part of something bigger.

3

❧

III. Po The Wizard

Po and Zap emerged from the lush forest, still buzzing with the excitement of their new adventure. The trees behind them swayed gently, and the sunlight filtering through the canopy cast a warm, golden glow on the forest floor. Po noticed broken branches and disturbed patches of grass near the edge of the trail. Strange, he thought, squinting into the thick foliage. Maybe it was just animals, but it made his heart beat a little faster. As they walked, the trail ahead of them seemed inviting, the sounds of birds chirping and leaves rustling filling the air.

"Well, that was quite a feast," Zap said, licking his lips as though he could still taste the food. "I could've stayed there a bit longer, but hey, adventure calls!"

Po smiled softly, the sense of support he'd felt from the villagers still warming him. "Yeah... It was nice, wasn't it?" He adjusted the strap of his backpack and glanced over his shoulder, almost missing the comforting trees of the village.

Just then, a voice echoed from the trees behind them. "You'll never make it far, you know. The world is far too dangerous for kids like you."

Po and Zap stopped in their tracks. Po turned slowly, eyes wide. "Did... Did that tree just talk?"

The tall tree with a crooked branch waved its leaves lazily. "What's the point? You'll probably get lost, or worse, fall into some trap. It happens all the time."

Zap's ears perked up, and he tilted his head. "Who's talking?"

A second tree, much sturdier and taller, leaned in closer. "Ignore him," it said in a deep, soothing voice. "The world is full of challenges, but those with sharp minds and brave hearts will always find a way."

Po blinked in amazement. "I've never seen talking trees before..."

The first tree rustled its leaves in a sigh. "What's the point of talking? No one listens."

Zap, never one to pass up a joke, grinned. "I think someone needs a nap!"

A third tree, its branches twisting playfully, chuckled. "If that tree took a nap, it'd probably dream of being a stick in the mud. Lighten up, would ya?" The tree gave a little shake, and a few leaves fluttered down. "You two seem fun. Where're you headed?"

Po, still fascinated by the strange conversation, smiled. "We're on a quest to save Princess Candy."

The wise tree's leaves rustled softly. "Ah, a noble journey indeed. Remember, young traveller, strength is not just in your arms, but in your mind. Think before you act, and you will find success where others falter."

Zap gave a playful bark. "Great advice! But I think I'll stick to action—thinking makes me sleepy."

Po laughed softly as they continued walking. The trees behind them offered final comments—some pessimistic, some wise, and some downright silly—but Po couldn't shake the feeling that the wise tree's words might come in handy soon.

As they walked further down the path, the forest thinned, and a large rock came into view. Perched atop it was a small, sprite-like figure, her shoulders trembling as she cried softly. Her wings drooped as if weighed down by her sadness. Po thought back to the broken branches and disturbed ground, feeling a nagging sense of caution, but her soft, trembling voice pushed it from his mind.

Po's heart immediately went out to her. "Are you okay?" he called, stepping closer with concern in his eyes.

The creature looked up slowly, wiping her eyes with a lavender paw. Her soft, fox-like features shimmered in the sunlight, framed by delicate, silver fur that caught the light. Large, round eyes, glistening with tears, met Po's, and her wings—small, translucent things that shimmered like glass—fluttered weakly. "No," she sniffled, her voice small and trembling. "I'm not okay... The bandits... they took my family's crystal pendant."

Zap's ears twitched as he narrowed his eyes. "Bandits?" His tone was a mix of curiosity and suspicion.

The creature nodded, her tears flowing again. "Yes, they ambushed me in the woods. It's a family heirloom, passed down for generations. Without it..." She hiccupped through her sobs. "Without it, I have no protection... Please, can you help me get it back?" Her trembling seemed to fade as she watched Po's reaction, a detail that slipped by as he was focused on her story.

Po exchanged a glance with Zap. He could already feel a pull to help the crying creature, her story tugging at his heartstrings. "We should help her," Po said, stepping forward with empathy. "It sounds important, and it's not right for her to be left without protection."

Zap raised an eyebrow, his tail flicking uncertainly. "Are you sure? This feels a little too convenient, don't you think?" Zap squinted at her tear-streaked face, noticing how quickly the tears seemed to vanish, but kept his doubts to himself. His tone was laced with scepticism, and his instincts told him there was more to this than met the eye.

Po, however, couldn't ignore the creature's pain. "If someone's in trouble, we can't just walk away."

The creature lifted her head and gave a hopeful, almost fragile smile. Her wings fluttered slightly, catching the sunlight. "Oh, thank you! You're so kind." She wiped her eyes again and sat up a bit straighter, her voice becoming steadier. "I'm Thistle, by the way."

"Thistle?" Po repeated, giving her a kind smile. "That's a pretty name. Don't worry, we'll help you get your pendant back."

Zap, however, was still watching her with a suspicious look in his eyes. He crossed his paws and muttered under his breath, "Thistle, huh? I've got my eye on you..."

Thistle either didn't hear him or chose to ignore Zap's comment, her voice now filled with new hope. "I can take you to where the bandits are hiding. It's not far," she promised, standing up and gesturing down a narrow, winding path leading deeper into the woods.

Po nodded without hesitation. "Lead the way."

Zap sighed, clearly not convinced, but padded along beside Po. "Alright, but I'm keeping my eye on her," he whispered to Po, his voice low. "Something feels off about this. We should be ready for anything."

Po shot him a sideways glance but said nothing. Despite his friend's warning, Po's kind nature wouldn't let him abandon someone in need, and Thistle's tears had seemed genuine enough.

They followed Thistle deeper into the woods, the trees growing taller and denser around them. The sunlight above dimmed as the branches overhead wove together, casting long shadows across the path. The air grew cooler, and a stillness settled over the forest that made Zap's fur bristle.

"So... these bandits," Zap asked, breaking the uneasy silence. "How many are we talking about here?"

Thistle glanced over her shoulder, her expression grim. "There are four of them. They're greedy, nasty creatures who've been hiding out for a long time. They'll take anything of value."

Zap's ears flattened. "Great," he muttered sarcastically. "Four against two. Just the kind of odds I like."

Po frowned, sensing the tension in Zap's voice. "We'll figure something out," he reassured, though he couldn't quite shake the growing unease in his own gut. Something about this felt off, but he didn't want to leave Thistle helpless.

Eventually, a small, rundown cottage came into view, nestled in a secluded grove. The wooden structure looked as though it hadn't been maintained in years, with ivy crawling up its sides and the roof sagging slightly. The windows were dark, and the air around it seemed colder, more ominous.

"This is it," Thistle whispered, her voice dropping to a trembling hush. "The bandits are inside."

Po felt his stomach tighten as he studied the cottage. Something wasn't right. The air was too still, and the eerie quiet pressed down on him like a weight.

Zap glanced around, his eyes narrowing suspiciously. "Doesn't look like anyone's home," he muttered. His fur stood on end as he sniffed the air. "I don't like this, Po. This feels like a trap."

Before Po could respond, the door of the cottage creaked open, and a low, sinister voice echoed from inside.

"You're right, dog. It is a trap."

Four gremlin-like creatures lunged from the shadows, their jagged teeth gleaming in the dim light. Po barely had time to react before they were both knocked to the ground, ropes wrapping tightly around their arms and legs. As Po struggled, the gremlins' leader—a snarling figure named Snagg—appeared in the doorway, sneering down at them.

"Well, well, what do we have here?" Snagg hissed, his yellow eyes glinting with malice. "Looks like we caught ourselves a couple of do-gooders."

Thistle, now standing with a wicked grin on her face, sauntered up to Snagg's side. "I told you they'd fall for it," she said, her voice now free of the trembling fear she had used earlier. "Pathetic, aren't they?"

Po's chest filled with shame, his cheeks reddening. How had he fallen for this so easily? He felt his heart sink, doubting his own judgment. Maybe Zap was right—he was too trusting. But how could he have known?

Zap groaned, rolling his eyes as the gremlins finished tying them up. "I knew it. Should've listened to me, Po."

Before Po or Zap could react, the bandits tied them up tightly with ropes, laughing as they struggled. Snagg and his crew began rummaging through Po's backpack, their eyes gleaming as they pulled out his belongings.

"Well, well, what do we have here?" Snagg grinned as he flipped through Po's science book. "Looks like we hit the jackpot."

Zap, always quick on his feet, smirked. "You better be careful with that book—it's no ordinary book. Po's a powerful wizard, and if you mess with that book, he'll turn you all into dusty boots, or maybe rusty buckets. Or... if he's feeling nasty... spoons!"

The bandits froze, exchanging nervous glances. "Spoons?" one of them muttered, looking horrified.

"Yeah," Zap continued, his voice full of mischief. "Imagine spending the rest of your life as a spoon. No one ever respects spoons. Everyone thinks forks are cooler. You don't want that, do you?"

Po couldn't help but smile slightly as Zap's bluff distracted the bandits. He leaned back against the wooden post, feeling the rough texture press against the ropes. He could almost hear Mrs. Yin's voice from science class echoing in his mind— "Friction creates heat, and heat can loosen or weaken materials." If he could generate enough friction, the rope might weaken just enough for him to slip free.

Carefully, Po began rubbing the rope against the post, moving his wrists slowly at first to create a steady rhythm. The rope scraped against the wood, and he felt it start to warm up. He glanced at the bandits, who were still bickering over Zap's ridiculous threats about becoming spoons.

"I'm telling you," Zap continued, rolling his eyes dramatically. "Spoons have the worst life. Just endless soup and cereal. Trust me, you don't want that."

Po gritted his teeth and kept rubbing the rope faster. His wrists started to ache, but he could feel the fibres fraying. The heat from the friction made the knots loosen slightly. Almost there...

The bandits, still arguing, had no idea what was happening. Snagg snarled at the others. "Enough with the spoons! Wizards aren't real, you idiots! It's just a book!"

Zap gasped dramatically. "Not real? Well, I guess you'll find out soon enough... unless you really want to be a rusty old bucket."

One of the bandits, wide-eyed and shivering, edged away from Po's backpack, clearly nervous. "I... I don't want to be a spoon..."

Finally, Po felt the ropes give way. With one swift motion, he slipped his hands free and quickly untied his feet. His heart raced with relief, but he didn't make a move to escape just yet. He had a better idea.

As quietly as possible, Po rummaged through his backpack and pulled out his instant camera, the one he used for his Art class. He remembered something he'd once read in the school library—a legend about a tribe that believed cameras could steal souls. That would be the perfect bluff to scare these bandits.

Standing tall, Po stepped forward, holding the camera up for the bandits to see. "You think Zap was joking about magic? Well, you're wrong."

The bandits froze, their wide yellow eyes staring at the strange object in Po's hands.

"This," Po said, his voice steady, "is how I trap souls."

Zap's eyes sparkled with amusement as he caught on to Po's plan. "Oh, yeah! You guys are in for it now. Po's going to trap your souls in that box. You'll be stuck forever as... well, I don't know. Paperweights? Fire pokers? Who knows what he'll make you into!"

Po pressed the camera's button, and the flash went off, bright and sudden in the dimly lit cottage. The bandits yelped in terror as Po held up the freshly printed photo.

"See this?" Po said, showing them the picture. "Your souls are now trapped in this photograph. If you don't change your ways—stop stealing and hurting others—I'll keep your souls trapped forever."

The bandits stared at the photograph, their faces pale and full of fear. Snagg's mouth dropped open, and the other bandits began trembling.

"W-we'll stop!" one of the bandits cried, his voice shaking. "We swear! We'll be good! Just... just don't keep our souls!"

Snagg, still trying to hold onto his tough demeanour, took a step back. "Y-yeah... We don't want any trouble. We'll stop. No more stealing!"

Zap grinned, clearly enjoying the moment. "You better! Or else Po will turn you all into soup spoons. That's the worst kind of spoon."

Po tucked the photo into his backpack, keeping his expression serious. "Good. Now, no more bad deeds. If I hear you've been up to trouble again, I'll keep your souls with me forever."

The bandits nodded furiously, their hands trembling as they backed away, clearly terrified. "No more bad stuff! We promise!"

Po gave them one final, stern look, then motioned for Zap to follow him. Together, they untied Zap's bindings and walked out of the cottage, leaving the bandits behind, still quivering in fear.

Once they were outside and the door had shut behind them, Po and Zap burst into laughter.

"That was incredible!" Zap said, his tail wagging furiously. "I thought I was good at bluffing, but you? Soul-trapping camera wizard? Genius!"

Po couldn't stop grinning. His heart was still racing, but this time it was from excitement, not fear. "I can't believe that worked!"

But as they walked, Po felt a pang of doubt. He'd trusted Thistle too easily. "Maybe I need to be more careful," he thought to himself. "Kindness is important, but maybe it's time to listen to my gut, too."

Zap held up his paw for a high-five. "We make a pretty great team, don't we?"

Po slapped his paw with a smile. "Yeah. We really do."

With the bandits behind them and a sense of accomplishment swelling in Po's chest, the two friends continued their journey down the path, feeling a little more confident—and a little more ready for whatever challenges lay ahead.

4

IV. Amberstone Ascent

Po and Zap left the dense embrace of the enchanted forest behind, feeling a surge of accomplishment after outsmarting the bandits. The forest opened to reveal a wide, golden meadow, stretching under the late afternoon sun. The light was warm here, softening the land and casting a gentle glow on the path ahead.

Zap bounded a few steps ahead, his tail wagging enthusiastically. "I think we're on a roll!" he called back. "Out of that forest, no more traps—maybe this journey isn't as tough as we thought!"

Po was about to agree when something caught his eye. A series of small hoof prints were embedded in the dirt path, fresh and dainty, heading in the same direction as them. He squinted down at the trail, curiosity piqued. "Zap, look," he murmured, pointing. "We're not the only ones passing through." Zap padded back to peer at the tracks, his nose twitching.

"A deer?" he guessed, though he seemed unsure. "Maybe." Po crouched, studying the prints more closely. They were distinct, carefully imprinted, and looked as if they were made by something deliberate and light-footed. "But these are more precise, like they're from a trained animal."

Zap shrugged, his eyes scanning the meadow ahead. "Well, if it's got small feet, it can't be that scary, right?" But his gaze flickered with an edge of wariness as he looked back toward the trees.

They walked on, the meadow around them quiet except for the soft buzz of insects and the occasional trill of a distant bird. Po couldn't shake the feeling of being watched, as if whoever or whatever had made those tracks was only a step ahead, just out of view.

"Something about this place feels different," Po murmured, tightening his grip on his backpack. He cast a glance over the golden fields, as if searching for any sign of movement. "Let's stay sharp, Zap."

As they moved away from the forest, the landscape began to change. The towering trees thinned out, giving way to rocky terrain. Soon, the path led them to a fork in the road, where a weathered signpost stood, its wooden signs pointing in three directions.

The first sign pointed back toward *Wilkwood*, the forest they had just left behind. The second sign pointed left and read *Amberstone Ascent*, and the third pointed right toward *The Sinking Marshes*.

Po studied the signs, scratching his head. "So, which way should we go, Zap?" Before Zap could answer, they both heard footsteps behind them. They turned, but no one was there. The path they had just walked was completely empty. Zap narrowed his eyes. "Did you hear that?" Po nodded slowly, still looking around. "Yeah, I did."

Suddenly, the sound of hooves clopping against the ground filled the air. They spun around again, and this time, saw a figure approaching—a man with a long white beard, riding a strange four-legged creature that looked like a donkey, but its ears were longer, and its fur seemed to shimmer faintly in the sunlight.

The old man waved as he drew closer. "Good day, travellers! Didn't mean to startle you. I'm just a humble merchant, making my way through the mountains. Care to take a look at my wares?"

There was something peculiar about his sudden appearance, but Po couldn't quite place it. His warm demeanour contrasted with his penetrating gaze, which seemed to search Po and Zap for something beyond curiosity.

Po and Zap exchanged glances, still slightly bewildered by the sudden appearance of the merchant. He hadn't been anywhere near them just moments ago, but here he was, cheerful and ready to do business.

Zap whispered to Po, "Where did he even come from?"

Po shrugged. "I have no idea, but... I guess it wouldn't hurt to see what he's selling."

The old man dismounted, moving with surprising agility for someone of his age. He opened a small, worn pack and laid out a few items on the ground in front of them.

There were only four items:

1. *A vial of sparkling blue liquid, glowing softly in the light.*
2. *A small but sturdy-looking sword, simple in design but sharp.*
3. *A rolled-up map, yellowed at the edges.*
4. *A small packet of crayons, bright and colourful but oddly out of place among the other items.*

Po crouched down, eyeing the items with curiosity. He picked up the vial of blue liquid, turning it in his hands. "What's this?" he asked.

The merchant scratched his beard thoughtfully. "That? Well, I'm not entirely sure. Could be a potion of sorts, could be something else entirely. Whatever it is, I'm sure it would have some

interesting effects." Zap snorted. "Yeah, interesting like turning us into frogs. Better not drink it, Po."

Zap then gestured toward the crayons, his tail wagging with amusement. "What about these? What kind of magic powers do the crayons have?"

The merchant blinked in surprise. "Oh, those? Erm, they're not magical. Those are my daughter's crayons. Must've fallen into my pack by accident."

Po chuckled but soon realized they had no money. "We'd love to buy something, but we don't have any money."

The merchant waved his hand dismissively. "No matter! I've heard of your quest. You're the ones who plan to save the princess, yes?"

Po blinked, surprised. "How did you—?"

The merchant grinned. "Word travels fast. You two have been making quite the impression. As a gesture of gratitude, you may take one item, free of charge."

As the merchant spoke, Po noticed a small pendant hanging from his neck, bearing an emblem that felt eerily familiar—a

symbol that tugged at his memory, but he couldn't quite place where he had seen it before.

Po and Zap looked at each other, unsure which item to choose.

"I mean, we can't take the crayons," Po said, smiling. "They belong to your daughter."

Zap shook his head. "And we're definitely not taking that potion. I'm not into random potions that could make us grow a second tail."

"So," Po said, looking between the last two items, "the sword or the map?"

Zap nodded. "The map would be helpful since we don't really know this place, but the sword would give us some protection. It's dangerous out here."

After a moment of consideration, Po decided. "We'll take the sword."

The merchant handed Po the small sword, its weight settling comfortably in his hand. "Good choice," the merchant said with a wink. "And remember, that sword has had many owners. It has a history, though some of its secrets only reveal themselves to those worthy of wielding it."

With that, the merchant mounted his creature again and rode off down the path, leaving Po and Zap standing at the crossroads.

Zap gave the merchant one last curious look as he disappeared down the road. "I don't know, Po—he didn't seem like your average travelling salesman."

"Well," Zap said after a moment, "We don't have a map, so which way should we go?"

"I'm not too keen on visiting anywhere with *sinking* in the name." Po quipped with a grin. Zap nodded. "Yeah, Amberstone Ascent it is."

Po and Zap made their way up the narrow, rocky path that wound its way up the side of the mountain. The climb was steep, and the path grew thinner as they ascended. The wind picked up, tugging at Po's clothes, and he could feel his muscles starting to ache from the effort.

"So," Po said between breaths, "what's the plan when we reach the princess? I mean, we've got this sword now, but... how are we supposed to fight the Shadow Twins? They're supposed to be powerful." Zap, however, wasn't paying attention. "Huh? Oh, sorry. I was thinking about those crayons. Weird that a guy that old has crayons for his daughter. Wouldn't she be, like, in her sixties or something?" Po sighed, feeling his energy waning. "Zap, can we focus? We need to figure out what we're going to do when we reach the princess."

But before they could discuss further, the path came to an abrupt halt. In front of them stood a giant, unmovable rock, completely blocking their way forward.

Po stared at it, his heart sinking. "Are you kidding me?" he muttered, his frustration building. "We climbed all the way up here for nothing?" A tight knot of self-doubt grew in his chest. Maybe he wasn't ready for this journey. The forest was one thing, but facing actual magic, curses, and a blocked path that had no clear solution made him feel out of his depth. "I can't do this," he thought, his grip on the sword loosening. Exhausted and frustrated, Po's anxious and pessimistic side began to creep back in. "I knew we should've taken the map! This sword is useless if we can't even get past a stupid rock!" Zap frowned, sensing his friend's frustration. "Hey, hey, it's okay. We'll figure something out. We always do." Po didn't respond, his mind clouded with irritation. Zap, thinking quickly, smiled. "You know what helps me when I'm stressed? Singing!" He began to hum a tune, his voice cheerful as he sang about their adventure so far.

♫ *Off to save the princess, we go! Tricked those bandits, can't beat Zap and Po!* ♫

As Po listened to the song, something clicked in his mind. The mention of their adventure reminded him of the flute that hung around his neck. He felt the wooden flute necklace resting against his chest and remembered what Habzar had said. "I've got an idea!" Po said suddenly, his eyes lighting up. He reached for the flute and brought it to his lips. The soft, soothing sound filled the air, and a gentle warmth spread across the rocky landscape. As the notes echoed through the mountains, the giant rock before them began to rumble. Slowly, it rolled to one side, revealing a narrow gap just large enough for them to squeeze through.

Po and Zap exchanged excited glances. "It worked!" Po

exclaimed; his earlier frustration forgotten. Zap grinned. "What are we waiting for? Let's go!"

They squeezed through the gap and found themselves in the hollow of the mountain. The narrow gap opened into a vast, dimly lit tunnel, and as Po and Zap stepped inside, they were immediately enveloped in a thick, swirling mist. It clung to their clothes and fur, making everything feel damp and cold. Their footsteps echoed softly off the stone walls, the only sound in the eerie silence that filled the hollow.

"I don't like this," Zap muttered, his tail lowered as he glanced around. "It's too quiet. And what's with all the mist?" Po was about to respond when something caught his eye—far ahead, through the mist, there was a faint, flickering golden glow. It pulsed softly, as if beckoning them closer.

"Look," Po said, pointing. "There's something up ahead." Zap squinted through the fog. "You think it's treasure? Gold? Let's check it out!"

The two of them moved forward cautiously, the glow growing brighter with each step. But as they approached, Po noticed something else—the temperature was rising. The deeper they ventured into the hollow, the hotter the air became, until sweat began to bead on Po's forehead and his shirt clung uncomfortably to his back.

"Is it just me, or is it getting... really hot in here?" Po asked, wiping his brow. Zap panted, his tongue lolling out. "Yeah, like a furnace. What do you think is causing it?"

"I don't know," Po admitted, "but we're about to find out."

Finally, they stepped into a larger chamber, the golden glow now bathing everything in its warm light. But their path was blocked by a massive stone door, ancient and imposing, with runes etched across its surface. The runes glowed faintly, the same golden hue as the light filling the chamber.

Zap stared up at the door, eyes wide. "Whoa. What is this place?" Po stepped closer, studying the runes. "It looks like some kind of puzzle... Maybe we have to figure it out to get inside."

Zap's ears twitched with interest. "A puzzle? Well, it can't be too hard. How do we solve it?" Po ran his fingers over the symbols, tracing their shapes thoughtfully. "It looks like we need to press these in the right order," he said, noticing how some of the runes were slightly raised. "But we have to figure out what the right order is..."

The two of them began to inspect the door more closely. Zap, as usual, threw out wild guesses, randomly suggesting combinations based on his whims. "What if we press them in order of size? Or maybe by how cool they look?" he suggested, his eyes gleaming with excitement.

Po rolled his eyes but couldn't help but smile at Zap's enthusiasm. "Let's try to think this through," he said, trying to focus. He squinted at the carvings, then noticed a pattern—the glowing runes formed the shape of a dragon in flight. "I think we need to follow the path of the dragon."

Zap leaned in closer, his face inches from the door. "A dragon, huh? That's pretty cool," he murmured, tracing the outline with his paw. "But how do we know where it starts and ends?"

Po stepped back, taking in the entire door. "Good question," he muttered. "Maybe there's a clue in the details." He scanned the

surrounding area, looking for anything that might indicate a starting point. His eyes landed on a small, barely noticeable mark at the dragon's tail. "There," he pointed. "I think we start here and follow the dragon's path to its head."

He carefully pressed the runes in a sequence that followed the shape of the dragon. With a low rumble, the stone door shuddered and slowly began to slide open, revealing what lay beyond. Po and Zap exchanged excited glances before stepping into the next

chamber. What they saw next took their breath away. The chamber beyond the door was massive, its ceiling so high that it disappeared into the darkness above. But what immediately caught their attention were the mountains of treasure that filled the

cavern. Piles of gold coins, glittering jewels, and shining goblets were stacked as far as the eye could see. Amulets, crowns, and gem-encrusted goblets lay scattered across the ground, as if carelessly discarded by some long-forgotten ruler.

Zap's eyes went wide, his jaw dropping in disbelief. "Po... are you seeing this?" Po could only nod, equally stunned. "We... we're rich."

Without hesitation, Zap leaped into one of the piles of gold, scooping up handfuls of coins and letting them fall through his paws. "We're rich! We could buy anything! This is amazing!"

Po laughed, feeling a surge of excitement. He picked up a glittering necklace and held it up to the light, admiring the way the jewels sparkled. "Look at this! It's beautiful. We could... we could buy a castle with this!"

Zap, now covered in gold dust, tossed a handful of coins into the air and grinned. "Or a whole fleet of ships! Or our own kingdom! The possibilities are endless!" For a moment, they were lost in their newfound wealth, playing and laughing like

children. They tossed coins at each other, admiring the treasure around them and imagining what they would do with it all. But their laughter was suddenly interrupted by a deep rumbling sound. Po froze, the necklace slipping from his fingers. "What... was that?"

The rumbling grew louder, and the ground beneath them began to tremble. Coins shifted and clinked together as something stirred beneath the treasure. Po and Zap stood perfectly still, eyes wide, as the treasure pile in front of them began to rise. And then, from beneath the mountain of gold, a massive shape emerged.

The treasure seemed to fall away like water as a massive dragon rose from the pile of gold. Its scales shimmered like molten metal, catching the golden light of the chamber. Gold coins clung to its body, and its eyes glowed a deep, furious red.

With a deafening roar, the dragon stretched its wings, sending a cascade of coins crashing to the ground. Flames flickered at the edges of its mouth, and its breath was hot enough to scorch the air around them.

Zap's ears flattened against his head. "Uh, Po? I think we woke something up..." Po's heart pounded in his chest as the dragon's gaze locked onto them, its eyes narrowing in rage. "Run!" he shouted, grabbing Zap by the scruff of his neck and pulling him toward the nearest pile of treasure for cover.

The dragon roared again, its voice shaking the very walls of the cavern. With a mighty swing of its tail, it sent gold and jewels

flying, clearing the space around it. And then, with a blast of fiery breath, it sent a jet of flames shooting across the chamber, narrowly missing Po and Zap.

They ducked behind a pile of treasure, gasping for breath. "What do we do?" Zap whispered, his voice trembling.

Po's mind raced. "We can't fight that thing... not like this." He peeked over the pile of gold, watching as the dragon's head swivelled back and forth, searching for them. Suddenly, Po remembered the sword they had taken from the merchant. His hand instinctively reached for the hilt. "The sword... maybe it can help us." Zap looked sceptical. "You think that little sword can take on a dragon?"

"It's our only chance," Po said, gripping the sword tightly. "I have to try." With the sword in hand, Po stood up, his heart pounding in his ears. The dragon saw him immediately, its eyes glowing with anger as it reared back, preparing to unleash another torrent of fire.

Before the dragon could strike, Po lifted the sword high, the blade catching the light of the dragon's fire. As the flames rushed toward him, the sword began to glow—a bright, blinding light that cut through the heat. The dragon recoiled, momentarily stunned by the light. Seizing the opportunity, Po lunged forward, aiming for the dragon's chest. The blade connected with the dragon's scales, and with a burst of energy, the sword seemed to absorb the dragon's fire, turning it into a brilliant flash of light. The dragon let out a pained roar, stumbling backward as the light from the sword grew even brighter. Po swung the sword again, this time striking the dragon's jaw. With a loud crack, one of the dragon's teeth flew out, landing with a thud on the cavern floor.

Po staggered back, the sword still glowing faintly in his hand. The dragon, now injured and weakened, glared at them one last time before retreating into the shadows, disappearing into the farthest corners of the cavern. For a long moment, Po and Zap stood in stunned silence, the echoes of the dragon's roar fading into the distance. "Did we... did we beat it?" Po asked, his voice shaky. Zap, still panting from the adrenaline, grinned. "I think you just injured it. But Po, that was incredible! You were like a knight or something!"

Po looked down at the sword, its glow fading as the room grew quiet again. "This sword... it's not just any sword." He thought back to the merchant's words: *only those worthy can uncover its secrets.* Was there more to this sword? A secret power he'd yet to discover? Po slipped it back into its sheath, feeling both grateful and a little unnerved.

Zap wagged his tail, nudging Po's side. "Told you the sword was a good choice! Who needs a map when you've got a magic sword?" They laughed together, though the weight of what had just happened still hung in the air. Po slipped the sword back into its sheath, feeling both relieved and a little more confident. The dragon may have been terrifying, but they had faced it and survived.

5

V. Shangri-La

After their victory over the dragon, Po and Zap stood in the stillness of the hollow. The air was cooler now, the treasure scattered around them glinting faintly in the fading light. Despite their exhaustion, Po couldn't help but feel the weight of the dragon tooth in his backpack, a tangible reminder of their daring escape. The tooth had fallen out during their encounter, and Zap, ever the practical one, had insisted on keeping it as a "cool memento."

"Come on, Po! We've got more climbing to do," Zap said cheerfully, bounding ahead over the uneven rocks.

Po sighed, glancing at the steep, jagged terrain in front of them. The climb looked challenging, but there was no other way out. The tunnel they had followed led them upward, and the path was becoming steeper with each step. Sharp rocks and narrow ledges made the ascent difficult, and Po found himself gripping the edges of the stone to avoid slipping.

"I feel like we've been climbing forever," Po muttered, pausing to catch his breath. His hands and knees were scraped from the rough surface. "Are we even close to the top?"

Zap, hopping easily from rock to rock, looked back and grinned. "Come on, Po! You just took down a dragon. A few rocks are nothing!"

Po smiled despite his exhaustion, taking another deep breath as he pulled himself higher up the slope. He knew Zap was right—the dragon was behind them now, and the only way forward was to keep going.

After several more minutes of climbing, Po finally hoisted himself up onto a wide ledge and stopped in his tracks. His eyes widened in awe. The narrow path they had followed through the mountain had opened into a wide plateau at the top of the mountain.

In front of them, a waterfall cascaded from a natural spring, its clear water tumbling into a sparkling pool below. Around the pool, the ground was lush with vibrant green grass and patches of flowers in every imaginable colour. The sun bathed everything in golden light, and the air felt warm and peaceful. Majestic animals wandered nearby—white deer, glimmering birds, and creatures that looked like a cross between rabbits and foxes, their fur shimmering in the sunlight.

"Did we just discover Shangri-La?" Po joked, a broad smile spreading across his face. For the first time since entering the mountain, he felt truly at peace.

Zap, tilting his head in confusion, glanced around. "Shangri-what? Is that a place around here?"

Po chuckled. "No, it's from a book. 'Lost Horizon.' Shangri-La is this mystical, peaceful place hidden in the mountains. It's fictional. But standing here, this place almost feels like it could be real."

Zap shrugged, not entirely sure what Po was talking about but clearly enjoying the beauty around them. "Well, I don't know about books, but I could hang out here forever. This place is amazing."

After a few moments of taking in the breathtaking view, Po wandered over to the edge of the plateau, where the water from the pool flowed over a cliff, creating a long waterfall that cascaded into the forest below. He peered over the edge, his stomach twisting nervously. The drop was steep and high, far too dangerous to climb down.

"Uh, Zap?" Po called, biting his lip. "How are we supposed to get down from here, wouldn't we get hurt if we jump down?"

Zap trotted over to join him, looking down at the waterfall with a mischievous gleam in his eye. "There's only one way to find out!"

Before Po could react, Zap leaped from the edge of the plateau, diving straight into the pool of water below with a splash.

"Zap!" Po shouted, his heart racing. He rushed to the edge, fear gripping him as he stared down at the water. "Zap! Are you okay?"

For a moment, there was no response. But then, Zap's head popped up from beneath the water, his fur soaked but his grin wide. "Come on, Po! The water's great!"

Zap shook the water from his fur, laughing. "See? Although... probably not the best idea, diving headfirst into who-knows-what."

Po took a deep breath, still feeling a knot of anxiety in his chest. "I can't believe I'm doing this," he muttered to himself.

Steeling himself, Po took a few steps back before running and leaping into the water. For a brief moment, he felt weightless as the wind rushed past him, and then he plunged into the cool, refreshing pool below.

When he resurfaced, he gasped for air, his body tingling from the adrenaline. He looked over at Zap, who was already paddling toward the edge of the pool, laughing.

"See? I told you!" Zap called. "You survived the dragon, the waterfall... we're practically invincible!"

Po couldn't help but laugh, the tension from the climb and the jump melting away. "Yeah, yeah. You were right."

They pulled themselves out of the water and collapsed onto the soft grass, both soaked but unharmed. For a moment, everything felt peaceful again.

As they lay on the grass, the sun warm on their faces, Po and Zap took in the beauty of the plateau. Everything seemed perfect—the animals frolicked nearby, the air was fresh and sweet, and the sound of the waterfall was soothing. It was as if they had stumbled upon a paradise.

Po's moment of peace was disturbed by a flicker at the edge of his vision. A slight change in the water's colour—it went murky, just for a split second. His stomach clenched, a faint chill creeping over his skin.

As they rested, Po noticed other peculiarities. The edges of the flowers in front of him seemed to flicker, as though the vibrant colours were fading in and out. He rubbed his eyes, thinking it was a trick of the light, but the flowers wilted for a split second before blooming again.

"Did you see that?" Po asked, sitting up.

Zap was rolling in the grass, unbothered. "See what? This grass is amazing, Po. You've got to try it."

Po frowned. His mind raced, trying to make sense of what he had seen. He bent down and touched one of the flowers. For a moment, it felt rough and dry, not at all like the soft, vibrant petals he had expected.

Disappointment twisted in his stomach. This whole place, so perfect and peaceful... were they walking into another trap?

Something wasn't right.

Before Po could investigate further, one of the small creatures nearby—a cute, furry animal with big eyes and a friendly expression—approached them. Its voice was soft and kind as it spoke. "You must be tired after your journey. Welcome to our peaceful haven."

Zap sat up, wagging his tail. "Oh, hey! A talking animal! This place just gets better and better."

The creature smiled sweetly. "Would you like me to show you something magical? There's a special place here, hidden just for travellers like you. You'll feel completely restored."

Po's unease deepened. He studied the creature closely, sensing that something wasn't quite right, but he couldn't put his finger on it. Everything seemed perfect—the vibrant colours, the sweet scent of flowers, the peaceful animals. But there was something... off.

He glanced around, still trying to shake the nagging feeling in his gut. And then, out of the corner of his eye, he noticed something unusual: a small sapling standing among the lush greenery.

Unlike everything else, the sapling looked too perfect, its leaves too vibrant, its bark unblemished. While the flowers had flickered earlier, and the air occasionally felt colder than it should, this sapling remained untouched by whatever small distortions Po had sensed.

Curiosity gnawed at him, and without fully understanding why, Po found himself drawn toward it. His feet carried him closer as if something was urging him forward. He didn't say anything to Zap, but his heart quickened as he reached out, his hand slowly extending toward the sapling.

As Po's fingers brushed against the smooth bark, the world around them shuddered.

The vibrant flowers around them began to wilt and crumble, the once-blue sky above them dimming to a sickly gray. The majestic animals that had been frolicking near the waterfall flickered and vanished, replaced by the decaying carcasses of creatures long dead. The once-green grass turned dry and brittle underfoot, and a foul stench filled the air, replacing the sweet scent of paradise.

Po's breath hitched, his heart racing as the entire illusion collapsed around them.

The creature that had been so kind and friendly twisted into something horrifying—a tall, shadowy figure with rotting features and glowing red eyes. The creature let out a low, sinister laugh as its true form revealed itself: a witch, cloaked in dark magic, her face contorted with malice.

Her voice grated like stones against metal as she sneered, "Such naive little travellers, oblivious to the dangers they are walking into."

"You thought you'd found a safe haven," the Witch hissed, her voice no longer gentle but dripping with venom. "But this place is mine. You will not leave here alive." With a flick of her hand, the once-cute animals around them reformed into shadow-like creatures, their forms warped and twisted with dark magic.

Before they could react, the shadow creatures lunged at them, their movements jerky and fast. Po's heart raced, panic setting in as they scrambled to their feet.

"We have to get out of here!" Po shouted, grabbing the flute from around his neck. He didn't know what to do, but he had to try something. Without thinking, he began to play the flute, hoping it would help.

As the soft, soothing sound filled the air, the shadow creatures froze in place, their dark forms trembling before turning to ash and crumbling away.

The Witch screamed, covering her ears. "What is that awful sound?! Stop it!"

Seizing the moment, Zap darted forward, biting down on the Witch's leg. She let out a furious cry, shaking him off and sending him tumbling to the ground.

Po scanned the area frantically, his eyes locking onto the sapling. It was the only thing that still seemed untouched by the chaos. "That's it," Po muttered, gripping his sword. "That's the source of her power."

But before Po could move, the Witch regained her composure, and the shadow creatures rose again, reforming from the ashes. They moved toward Po, faster this time, their red eyes glowing.

Desperate, Po played the flute again, the creatures disintegrating once more. But the Witch wasn't giving up. She turned her attention to Zap, her eyes narrowing.

"Let's see how fast you are, little dog," she hissed, lunging toward him.

Zap, quick on his feet, dodged her attack, zigzagging around the plateau with a mischievous grin. "Come and get me!" Zap shouted over his shoulder, darting between the crumbling rocks with ease, his movements quick and precise. He led the Witch on a frantic chase, weaving through the dead landscape with careful precision.

While the Witch was distracted chasing Zap, Po ran toward the sapling. His heart pounded as he raised his sword and sliced through the branches, cutting them off cleanly. Then, with all his strength, he pulled the sapling from the ground, unearthing its roots.

Suddenly, the air around them grew still. For a moment, Po feared nothing had changed. But then, like the first signs of dawn after a long night, the world around them began to shift.

The dead trees shuddered and creaked, their withered branches filling with new leaves, while the brittle grass turned green again, shooting up from the once-barren soil. Flowers began to bloom, not as vividly as they had in the illusion, but in soft, natural colours—white, yellow, lavender—filling the air with the gentle scent of nature's rebirth.

The pool at the base of the waterfall cleared its murky waters returning to a fresh, crystal-clear blue. The decayed animals did not return, but in their place, birds began to sing, and small creatures emerged from the forest's edges, timid but curious.

Po stood there, panting, the uprooted sapling still clutched in his hand. The world around them was now real, imperfect but full of life.

Zap trotted back to Po, shaking his fur dry and grinning. "Well, that was close."

But before Po could respond, the Witch's eyes glowed a deep red, and a grim smile twisted her face as she spoke one final word: "This isn't over. The darkness is coming." Then, with a final burst of dark energy, she vanished into the shadows, leaving a cold chill lingering in the air.

Po looked around, still trying to process what had happened. His chest heaved with the adrenaline of their escape, and his heart slowly began to steady. But one question still lingered.

"Zap," Po said, his voice cautious. "Where did the Witch go?"

Zap blinked, then looked around. "Huh... I dunno. One moment she was chasing me, and the next... she was just gone."

Po frowned, scanning the now peaceful landscape. The Witch, the creatures, the illusion—they had all vanished, as though they'd never been there at all.

"Do you think we—" Po started, but he stopped himself. Whatever had happened, the plateau was safe again, and that was all that mattered.

The sun, now fully restored to a gentle warmth, shone over the renewed land. Just as Po was about to suggest they rest for a bit, a familiar voice broke the calm.

"Well, well, well... if that wasn't one of the most interesting things I've seen in quite some time."

Po and Zap spun around to see the mysterious travelling merchant, his long white beard flowing down his chest as he sat atop his strange, donkey-like creature. The same twinkle of mischief shone in his eyes as he gazed down at them.

Zap's ears perked up. "You saw that? Were you here the whole time?"

The merchant nodded, his grin widening. "Indeed, I was. Watched the whole thing. Quite the show, if I do say so myself."

Po frowned, confused. "But... if you were here, why didn't you step in and help?"

The merchant gave a casual shrug. "I had a feeling you two could handle it. And look! You did. Quite impressively, might I add."

Zap's tail wagged with pride, but Po still looked suspicious. "But you could've at least warned us."

"Now where's the fun in that?" the merchant said with a wink.

Po let out a small sigh and shook his head, feeling like he should've known better by now than to expect straight answers from the man. But before Po could say anything else, the merchant's gaze shifted to the sapling root still clutched in Po's hand. His eyes widened with interest, and he leaned forward, eyeing it as though it was some rare treasure.

"My, my, what have we here?" the merchant said, rubbing his hands together. "Is that the root of the sapling from this cursed land?"

Po glanced down at the root, still dirty from where he had yanked it from the ground. "Uh... yeah. Why?"

The merchant's face lit up. "I'll make you a deal, young man. Trade me that root, and I'll let you choose one of my items. It's a fair trade, wouldn't you say?"

Zap blinked in confusion. "Wait... you want this root? Why? What could you possibly want with a sapling root?"

The merchant waved a hand as if it were obvious. "It makes a delightful soup. Best flavour in all the realms. But you don't need to worry about that—what matters is, I'll give you something in return." He hopped down from his mount and spread out his wares once again.

The same three items lay before them: the vial of blue potion, the map, and the box of crayons. However, something caught Zap's eye.

"Hey, wait a second," Zap said, narrowing his eyes at the box. "One of the crayons is missing!"

The merchant chuckled softly, scratching his beard. "How unusual. I wonder where it went."

Zap shrugged. "Yeah, nobody likes the orange crayon anyway. It's like the bounty of the crayon family."

Po shook his head, half-smiling at the oddity of the merchant and his strange explanations. He looked at the items, knowing there wasn't much to deliberate on this time.

"The map," Po said confidently, pointing toward it. "We'll take the map."

Zap nodded in agreement, not even considering the other items this time. "Yeah, definitely the map. I've had enough of mysterious potions and crayons."

The merchant clapped his hands, clearly pleased. "A wise choice, indeed!" He picked up the map and handed it to Po in exchange for the sapling root. Po hesitated for a moment, then gave the root to the merchant, wondering how anyone could be so excited about soup made from something they had just fought so hard to destroy.

The merchant, his mood lighter than ever, tucked the root away and mounted his creature once again. "Well, travellers, I bid you farewell—for now. I've no doubt our paths will cross again soon."

With a small wave, he clicked his tongue, and his strange steed trotted off down the path, disappearing into the distance almost as quickly as he had appeared.

Po unrolled the map, carefully spreading it out between his hands. The parchment was old but well-preserved, the lines of the land drawn with intricate detail. It didn't take long for him to spot their current location—a small marking of a mountain near a waterfall.

"Here we are," Po said, pointing to the spot. "At the top of the mountain."

Zap, peering over his shoulder, wagged his tail in excitement. "Great! So how do we get down?"

Po scanned the map for a moment before his eyes landed on a clear path descending from the mountain. "It looks like there are two places at the foot of the mountain that we can visit."

He ran his finger over the markings. One route was labelled Solaris Athenaeum, and the other, Lumisage Grove. Beside each name, there were small symbols: for Solaris Athenaeum, a building with the sun above it, and for Lumisage Grove, mushrooms scattered along a forest path.

Zap tilted his head, his expression puzzled. "Solaris what? Lumisage where? These words make no sense."

Po furrowed his brow. "Well, the symbols are clues. Solaris Athenaeum looks like some kind of building—maybe a temple or a weather station. And Lumisage Grove has mushrooms... which means it might be a forest."

Zap's ears perked up as he glanced back at the map. His eyes widened as he noticed something else. "Wait, Po! There's another option here—Mercury Station." He jabbed at a small symbol near the base of the mountain: a train.

"A train?" Po asked, squinting at the map. Sure enough, the symbol was there. "That could be interesting."

Zap wagged his tail. "Yeah, a train sounds fun! Much better than whatever those other two places are."

Po chuckled, shaking his head. "Let's get off this mountain first. We can decide which path to take once we're down there."

Zap nodded eagerly. With the map in hand, they began their descent. The path was much smoother than the way they had come up—wider, less rocky, and with a clear route winding its way down the mountainside.

As they descended, Po couldn't help but feel a growing sense of excitement. Zap on the other hand was humming away and singing about their latest triumph.

♫ Beat a dragon, took its tooth,
Jumped from a waterfall, fearless and smooth,
Ended the Witch's curse, broke her dark spell,
Now we're heroes, with stories to tell! ♫

6

VI. Flying Trains

Po and Zap descended the mountain, their boots crunching softly on the gravel as the day began to fade into night. The sky above was a mix of deep oranges and purples, quickly giving way to a darker shade as the stars began to peek through.

At the foot of the mountain, Po opened the map, the parchment damp from the mist clinging to the forest floor. He squinted at the dim light, tracing the lines from their current location. "Alright," he muttered, "let's figure this out."

Zap, peering over Po's shoulder, tilted his head, eyebrows furrowed in confusion. "So... what's next, Po? Where are we going?"

"Good question," Po said, focusing on the words printed along the path ahead. "We've got Solaris Athenaeum up ahead."

Zap blinked. "Okay, Po, tell me this. What in the world is a Solaris Athenaeum?"

Po grinned, happy to have a moment to show off his knowledge. "Well, let's break it down. 'Solaris'—that's easy. It's got to do with the Sun or Fire. You know, like solar power."

Zap nodded along, pretending to understand. "Got it. Hot stuff."

"And then there's 'Athen'," Po continued. "That reminds me of Athens, the ancient Greek city."

Zap looked puzzled. "Ancient Greece? What does that have to do with fire?"

Po paused for a moment, thinking hard. "Well... maybe not directly. But then there's the ending: '-eum'. I've only seen that at the end of words like museum or colosseum."

Zap's eyes lit up as understanding—or at least, his version of it—dawned on him. "Oh! So, it's a museum about the weather in Greece!"

Po stopped mid-thought, giving him a confused look. "Wait, what? How did you get that from—"

Zap nodded confidently, as if he'd cracked the code. "You said sun, you said Greece, and then something about a museum. So, it's obviously where they store all the Greek weather. You know, sunny skies, clear beaches, and all that. Probably a room full of sunshine."

Po groaned, trying not to laugh. "No, Zap. It's not a museum about the weather."

Zap shrugged nonchalantly. "Could've fooled me. With a name like that, I bet it's where they keep the sun itself. What else would you do with a name like Solaris Athenaeum?"

Po, still chuckling from Zap's wild interpretation, shifted his focus back to the map. "Look here," he said, pointing. "There's Lumisage Grove on the way to Solaris Athenaeum. It's actually part of the route."

Zap scratched his ear thoughtfully. "So, the mushrooms aren't a destination, they're just... like a snack along the way?"

Po shook his head, grinning. "Sort of. But look, we can skip the grove entirely if we take the train from Mercury Station." He traced the line from the station, leading directly to Solaris Athenaeum. "The railroad is the direct route."

Zap, now eyeing the sky as the first raindrops began to fall, perked up. "I say we take the train. I mean, why walk when we can ride? And besides..." he paused as more droplets began to hit the map, "mushrooms are gross!"

Po glanced up, noticing the clouds rolling in, dark and heavy. The drizzle quickly turned into a steady downpour, soaking the ground and them along with it.

"Let's get moving," Po muttered, tucking the map away as they both began a brisk walk toward Mercury Station.

Along the path, a sudden rustling in the trees caught Po's attention. He froze, his heart racing. Was it just the wind, or...? The noise faded as quickly as it had come, leaving Po with an uneasy feeling. He glanced back over his shoulder, wondering if someone—or something—was watching them in the dark.

By the time they reached Mercury Station, the rain had become relentless, pouring down in thick sheets that made it hard to see more than a few feet ahead. The railroad stretched into the distance, glistening with water under the moonlight. It was quiet—eerily quiet, except for the sound of rain drumming against the wooden platform.

In front of them, a small waiting area building stood. The inside was lit dimly, the yellowish glow from old oil lamps spilling onto the platform. Po and Zap hurried inside, grateful for the shelter.

Po shook off his cloak, droplets of water scattering onto the wooden floor. "Finally, shelter," he said, setting his backpack down and pulling the map out again to dry it off.

Zap, meanwhile, hopped onto one of the wooden benches lining the walls. He stretched out comfortably, letting out a long sigh of relief. "I could get used to this."

As he glanced around, his eyes landed on a schedule board nailed to the wall. His brow furrowed. "Says here the next train is on... Wednesday."

Po paused, mid-motion, and glanced over. "Wednesday?"

Zap nodded. "Yep."

Po, his clothes now mostly dry, spotted something. He moved over to the corner of the waiting area, his gaze settling on a tall, antique grandfather clock.

The clock stood taller than Po, made of rich, dark wood with intricate carvings of leaves and vines winding along its frame. It looked out of place in the otherwise simple station, its craftsmanship far more ornate than the plain wooden benches.

Po's eyes were drawn to the clock face, which was unlike any other he'd seen. Instead of numbers, the face displayed the days of the week, with a single hand slowly ticking along. It was currently resting on Tuesday, its slow, rhythmic ticking filling the room.

The pendulum swung lazily back and forth inside the glass case, the soft sound of ticking mixing with the gentle patter of rain outside.

"Hey, Zap, look at this," Po called, still studying the clock. "It doesn't show the time... it shows the days."

Zap hopped off the bench, padding over to Po's side. He squinted at the clock. "That's... strange. But also, kind of helpful, I guess. At least we know what day it is."

Po chuckled, nodding.

As the two settled back onto the benches, the rain pounding harder against the windows, Zap's eyes drifted toward the railroad outside once again. His tail twitched with curiosity. "So, Po, what kind of train do you think is going to show up?"

Po, still staring absently at the clock, glanced over. "I dunno. Probably just a normal train."

Zap, clearly unsatisfied with that answer, smirked. "A normal train? In a place like this? No way. I bet it's going to be something wild. What if it's a magic train that doesn't even need tracks? Maybe it just flies!"

Po raised an eyebrow, intrigued but amused. "A flying train?"

Zap nodded, grinning. "Yeah! Or maybe it's a train made of clouds, and we just float the whole way. No tickets needed, because the wind just carries us wherever we need to go!"

Po couldn't help but laugh. "Zap, I think you've got the wrong idea about trains."

But Zap, as always, wasn't done yet. "Or wait! What if it's a living train? Like, it's got a face and can talk! You know, like those talking trains from the stories."

Po shot him a bemused look. "I think you've been reading too many picture books."

Po leaned back, clearing his throat, ready to shift into teacher mode. "Actually, do you even know how steam trains work?"

Zap tilted his head, genuinely curious. "Uh... no. But I feel like you're going to tell me."

Po nodded, smiling. "Exactly. See, a steam engine works by heating up water to create steam. The steam builds up pressure in the boiler and pushes the pistons, which make the wheels turn."

Zap's eyes widened, as if he had just discovered the meaning of life. "So, it's like... a big metal teapot on wheels?"

Po laughed. "Kind of! But the boiler's a lot bigger than a teapot, and they use coal or wood to keep the fire going. The steam runs through pipes, and the pressure moves the whole thing. That's how trains used to run."

Zap, still absorbing the information, paused thoughtfully. "Huh. So, no flying trains, then?"

Po shook his head, grinning. "Sorry, no flying trains."

As the room grew quiet, Po's thoughts drifted back to everything they had faced. He couldn't help but wonder what was still ahead—the Shadow Twins, the castle, and who knew what else. A shiver ran through him as he thought about the dark magic they'd encountered so far. Was he truly ready for this?

Zap, noticing the change in Po's mood, tilted his head. "Hey, what's with the face? You look like you just swallowed a lemon."

Po sighed softly, his voice quieter now. "I don't know, Zap... it's just... everything we've been through so far. I keep thinking about what's next. What if I'm not ready to face the Shadow Twins? I'm not a hero, Zap. I'm just... me."

Zap's ears twitched as he sat up, sensing Po's seriousness. "You're worried, huh?"

Po nodded, staring down at his hands, picking at a loose thread on his shirt. "Yeah. I mean, I know we've gotten this far, but what if it's too much for us? I've been lucky so far... but what if I make a mistake when it really matters?"

Zap frowned slightly. "A mistake? Po, you've been doing great! You took down a dragon, you figured out how to beat the witch, and you're the one with all the brains when it comes to reading maps and solving puzzles."

Po managed a small smile at Zap's encouragement, but the doubt lingered. "I guess. But what if I let you down? What if I let everyone down? I'm not always sure I know what I'm doing..."

Zap hopped down from the bench and sat next to Po, nudging him playfully with his shoulder. "Listen, Po, you're way tougher than you think. And smarter. You've handled everything that's come our way. I wouldn't have made it this far without you."

Po smiled a little more at that. "Yeah, but your plan is usually just to wing it. I'm not sure that's the best strategy."

Zap grinned, the mischief returning to his eyes. "Hey, winging it has worked so far, hasn't it? You worry too much. You've got this, Po. We'll figure it out together. You've got me, I've got you, and we've got a magic sword and a flute. Plus, we're headed to a fancy-sounding place. What could go wrong?"

Po laughed, shaking his head. "You're impossible, you know that?"

Zap puffed out his chest proudly. "Impossibly brilliant."

Po leaned back on the bench, the sound of the rain against the window suddenly more comforting. Maybe Zap was right. They had come this far together, and no matter what happened next, they would face it like they always did—side by side.

"As long as we stick together," Po said, his voice lighter now, "we'll figure it out."

Zap grinned, "That's the spirit! Now, let's get to that museum of sunshine or whatever it is."

Po chuckled, the last of his tension melting away for the moment. He didn't have all the answers, but with Zap by his side, maybe he didn't need to. They'd find their way, one step at a time.

With the tension between them eased, Zap's natural energy quickly returned. He hopped back onto the bench, tail wagging and eyes twinkling mischievously.

Zap sat up straighter and cleared his throat dramatically. "It's just a theory, but I bet there'll be floating tracks and wings on the engine. We'll soar over the mountains like eagles, gliding through the clouds, racing to Ancient Greece—past all the philosophers and statues!"

With a wink, Zap launched into an impromptu song, his voice playful and exaggerated:

♫ Flying trains to Ancient Greece,
With golden wings that never cease,
Past sunny skies and statues tall,
Racing through the clouds, we'll see it all! ♫

Po chuckled but found himself tapping his foot to the rhythm of Zap's silly song. Without thinking much of it, Po reached for the flute hanging around his neck. As Zap continued his ridiculous lyrics, Po lifted the flute to his lips, and soon enough, began to play along to the melody of the song.

The tune was light and carefree, matching Zap's whimsical words. The sound of the flute blended perfectly with Zap's cheerful singing, and for a moment, it felt like they were just two friends enjoying a bit of fun in the middle of a stormy night.

♫ Trains with wings and sails so bright,
Off to battle in the night!
We'll find the sun, we'll beat the rain,
We'll chase the skies with our flying train! ♫

As the music and song filled the small waiting area, something magical stirred around them. The soft glow of the oil lamps seemed to brighten, and a whistle echoed in the distance—so faint at first that they almost didn't notice it.

But as Po continued to play, the whistle grew louder, and Zap's singing faltered. He glanced out the window, ears twitching.

"Uh, Po... I think that's a real train."

Po lowered the flute, mid-note, as they both turned their attention to the platform outside. Through the rain and fog, the unmistakable outline of a black steam train came into view, its engine puffing thick clouds of smoke into the night air. The train pulled into the station with a long, echoing whistle.

Both Po and Zap froze as they heard a deep, booming voice call out through the rain:

"All aboard for Solaris Athenaeum!" Their eyes widened in unison, and without wasting another second, they scrambled off the bench.

"The train's here!" Zap exclaimed, excitement bubbling in his voice.

They rushed toward the train's door, its metal frame glistening under the glow of the station lights. As they reached the entrance, the door swung open, revealing a familiar face.

Standing there, wearing a crisp conductor's uniform, was none other than Habzar.

"Habzar?!" Po and Zap exclaimed together.

Habzar gave them a cheerful smile and tipped his conductor's cap. "Evening, lads! Hop on board. We've got quite the journey ahead."

Po blinked in surprise, still processing the sight of Habzar dressed like a proper conductor. "What are you doing here? I thought you were back in the village!"

Habzar chuckled, stepping aside to let them board. "Oh, this? Well, every inhabitant of Princess Candy's kingdom has a job, and mine just happens to be running this fine railway." He gave them a wink. "Keeps me busy."

Zap, still half-drenched from the rain, shook himself dry as he hopped onto the train, peering around in awe. "This place is fancy!"

As Po stepped up, Habzar pulled out a small notebook and a pen. "I can't let you travel without a ticket, now, can I?" He scribbled something quickly on two train tickets and handed them to Po, who accepted them with a raised brow.

"This one's on me," Habzar said with a grin, tucking his pen back into his pocket. "First-class service for the heroes who'll save the princess!"

Po smiled, sliding the tickets into his pocket. "Thanks, Habzar."

"No need to thank me, boys," Habzar replied, tipping his cap again. "And don't worry, I'll be keeping an eye on you two. Always have, in a way. There's a lot more to this journey than you know." He winked again, leaving Po wondering what he meant as they found their seats.

With that, Po and Zap entered the train, finding the interior grander than anything they could imagine. The plush seats, soft lighting, and polished wood gave the cabin a warm, welcoming feel—nothing like the damp, cold station they'd been stuck in just moments ago.

As the train began to pull out of Mercury Station, the steady hum of the engine filled the air, and the rhythmic clacking of the wheels on the tracks created a soothing melody. The rain began to lighten as the train chugged along, and through the windows, they could see the storm clouds starting to clear, revealing patches of starry skies.

Zap settled comfortably into one of the seats, letting out a contented sigh. "I gotta say, Po... a flying train would've been cool, but this is pretty nice too."

Po chuckled, shaking his head as he leaned back in his seat. "Yeah, I think we're good without the wings."

But as the train picked up speed, it gave a sudden, unexpected jolt. Po glanced out the window nervously, catching a glimpse of the trees passing in the darkness. "Did you feel that?" he asked, looking over at Zap.

Zap shrugged, unfazed. "Probably just getting up to speed. But... maybe it's a reminder, you know? We're getting closer to something big. Shadow Twins, princesses, spooky stuff—I'm ready."

Po nodded, feeling the same sense of anticipation. The train sped along, heading toward Solaris Athenaeum, and with each mile they travelled, the sense of adventure grew. The worries Po had felt earlier seemed to slip away, carried off by the steady motion of the train and the clearing skies.

7

❧

VII. The Library

The train ride had been peaceful, and as the weather cleared, Po and Zap felt lighter, their worries melting away with the rain. Before long, the train slowed, the soft clanking of the wheels on the tracks gradually fading until it came to a full stop at Solaris Athenaeum Station.

Po and Zap stepped off the train and immediately took in the sight of a massive, circular building looming ahead of them. It was old—older than anything Po had ever seen—with large stone walls and turrets that rose up into the misty sky. In front of the building stood two giant doors, heavy and wooden, with intricate carvings that looked worn from centuries of use.

Po stepped forward and pushed against one of the doors. It groaned under its weight as he heaved it open. "It's a bit heavy," Po muttered, struggling slightly before the door finally creaked open just enough for them to squeeze through.

The moment they stepped inside, they were greeted by an overwhelming sight—rows upon rows of bookshelves, stretching out into the distance and disappearing into the gloom. The ceiling seemed impossibly high, and as Po looked up, he counted seven floors, all lined with more shelves filled with books.

"This place is incredible," Po whispered, eyes wide with awe. "It's a library."

Zap, on the other hand, seemed less impressed. "Yeah, yeah. Where's all the sunshine? I thought this was supposed to be Solaris-*something*."

Po chuckled as they walked deeper into the library, their footsteps echoing in the vast, empty space. They soon came across a large signpost, its letters faded but still legible, pointing out the various sections of the library. Po squinted as he read them aloud.

"Ancient Recipes... Herbology... Modern History... Dragon Studies..." Po's finger ran down the list until he spotted something interesting. "And look here: Dark Magic Archives, on the fourth floor."

Zap crossed his arms. "Dark Magic, huh? That sounds like bad news."

Po nodded thoughtfully. "Maybe. But we're going to face Shadow Magic, right? This might be the only place where we can find something useful."

Zap sighed. "If we find a *Light Magic Archives*, let's go there next, okay?"

They made their way up the spiral staircase, the steps creaking under their weight as they ascended to the fourth floor. As they entered the Dark Magic Archives, they were met with rows of ancient, dusty books. The air felt heavier here, thick with the weight of forgotten knowledge.

Zap wrinkled his nose. "Smells like an old attic in here."

Po scanned the shelves, running his fingers along the spines of the books. Many of the titles were faded, barely readable. One caught his eye: *The Void's Whisper*. He pulled it off the shelf, flipping through the pages. Most of it was cryptic, filled with spells and notes written in strange, illegible handwriting.

Zap peered over Po's shoulder. "Anything useful?"

"Not yet," Po muttered, placing the book back and pulling another one down. "We need something that deals with Shadow Magic."

After what felt like ages of searching, Po's eyes finally landed on a worn, leather-bound book titled *Defence Against the Shadows*. His heart skipped a beat. "I think I've found something!"

He opened the book, and together, they skimmed through the pages. Inside were descriptions of shadow creatures, their strengths, and most importantly, their weaknesses. One passage caught Po's attention:

Shadows fear their own reflection, for in the light, they are revealed to be nothing.

Zap grinned. "Fear their own reflection? The Shadow Twins must be ugly then."

Po giggled, feeling a more hopeful. "This could help us when we face the Shadow Twins. We'll need to use light and reflection to fight them."

Just as they were about to read more, the sound of soft footsteps echoed through the archives. Po and Zap looked up, startled, as a tall figure approached from the far end of the aisle.

A woman stepped into the dim light, her skin a pale shade of green, her long black hair tied loosely behind her, and her round, thin-framed glasses gleaming in the shadows. She smiled softly as she approached them.

"Ah, we don't often have visitors in the Dark Magic Archives," she said, her voice smooth and melodic. "What brings you here?"

Po and Zap exchanged glances, unsure of how to respond at first. The woman seemed calm, friendly even, but her sudden appearance in such a dark place made them wary.

Zap, ever the blunt one, raised an eyebrow. "And who are you?"

The woman smiled, adjusting her glasses slightly. "I'm the Librarian. I keep the knowledge here... well-preserved. It's rare to have visitors, especially such... polite ones."

Po's curiosity got the better of him. "Polite ones? Have there been others?"

The Librarian's expression darkened slightly as she nodded. "Yes, a group of rather unpleasant individuals. They came a while ago, made quite a mess of the sixth floor... and even threatened me when I asked them to clean up."

Zap's ears perked up. "Threatened you? That's rude."

Po, feeling it wasn't their place to pry, simply said, "That sounds awful. I'm sorry you had to deal with that."

The Librarian's smile returned, her eyes softening. "No need to apologize. I'm just glad to meet some friendlier visitors. What brings you here?"

Po explained their quest to save Princess Candy and defeat the Shadow Twins. The Librarian listened carefully, her expression growing thoughtful.

"Well," she said after a moment, "perhaps I can help you. There's something on the ground floor you might find interesting."

The Librarian led them back down the stairs, her long purple robes brushing the floor as they followed her through the maze of shelves. Eventually, they reached a small, unassuming section of the library. The Librarian ran her fingers along the spines of the books, stopping at one in particular: "Keys: A Pathway to Success."

She pulled the book from the shelf, and with a soft rumble, the entire bookshelf shifted forward, then slid to the side, revealing a hidden passage behind it.

Zap's eyes widened. "Well, that's convenient."

The Librarian smiled. "This passageway leads directly to the dungeons of the Shadow Towers, where the Shadow Twins reside. Be careful, though. It's not an easy journey."

Zap, his tail wagging slightly, looked at Po. "I like this place. Secret doors and shortcuts? It's like a maze full of cheat codes."

Po chuckled, feeling the weight of the moment but appreciating Zap's light-heartedness.

They descended the narrow stone steps, candles along the walls lighting up as they went. The air grew cooler, and their footsteps echoed in the silence.

"So, how do we even know who the Shadow Twins are when we see them?" Zap asked, glancing around. "You think they'll be wearing name tags or something?"

Po smirked. "I doubt it. We'll figure it out."

They walked in silence for a while, and Po adjusted his backpack, feeling the familiar weight of the dragon tooth still inside. "This thing is starting to feel heavy again."

Zap groaned. "Tell me about it. And I'm getting hungry again."

Just as the conversation started to ease the tension, the sound of footsteps echoed behind them. Po and Zap froze, spinning around to see the familiar figure of the travelling merchant approaching them, his trusty mount at his side.

Zap's eyes narrowed. "Oh, c'mon! This guy again?!"

The merchant grinned, tipping his hat as he approached. "Heard your little song about trains. Catchy tune, really."

Zap blinked in surprise, then muttered, "Wait... how do you know about—oh, never mind."

The merchant gave a sly smile and looked them both over. "How about a little game? Solve my riddle, and I'll let you take one of my remaining items." He gestured to the blue potion and the box of crayons he still carried with him.

Po nodded, intrigued. "What's the riddle?"

The merchant cleared his throat, his eyes gleaming with mischief as he began:

> *I fly without wings, I cry without eyes,*
> *Wherever I go, darkness flies.*
> *Though I carry no shadow, I move with might,*
> *And bend to no creature, not even light.*

Zap blinked. "That... was confusing."

Po furrowed his brow, concentrating hard. He repeated the riddle quietly to himself: "Fly without wings... cry without eyes... darkness... no shadow... what moves with might but isn't affected by light?" He rubbed his temples, deep in thought.

The merchant stood patiently, but the smirk on his face showed he was enjoying Po's frustration. After a few moments, Po perked up, eyes wide with realization.

"It's got to be the wind!" Po said confidently. "The wind flies without wings, and it doesn't have eyes, but it can make things move or bend."

Zap gave him a sideways glance. "Really? That's your guess?"

The merchant chuckled softly. "A good guess," he said, "but not quite right."

Po's face fell, and he let out a frustrated sigh. "But that made sense..."

The merchant leaned in slightly, looking Po in the eye with a mix of amusement and sympathy. "I'll give you another chance. One more guess."

Po frowned, his mind racing. He went over the riddle again, trying to piece together the clues. But nothing else was coming to him. He felt stuck, frustration bubbling up inside him.

Before Po could speak again, Zap piped up, his ears twitching with excitement. "Wait, wait! I know this one!"

Po blinked, surprised. "You do?"

Zap nodded. "Yeah, I've heard this kind of riddle before! It's the moon, right? It doesn't have wings, but it moves across the sky, and it reflects light without casting its own shadow. Plus, the whole crying without eyes thing—like how the moon influences the tides!"

The merchant's grin widened. "Very good, my friend. The moon is the correct answer!"

Po stared at Zap, amazed. "How did you...?"

Zap shrugged casually, puffing out his chest a little. "I might not know much about books, but riddles? I've got a few tricks up my sleeve."

Po shook his head, smiling. "I can't believe you solved that."

Zap winked. "I surprise myself sometimes."

The merchant, still grinning, presented the two items once again. "As promised, you may choose one of these two items—the blue potion or the crayons."

Po and Zap exchanged a quick glance, and without hesitation, Po pointed to the blue potion. "We'll take the potion."

The merchant nodded and handed over the sparkling blue vial. "A wise choice. Though its exact properties are... well, let's just say, they're interesting."

Zap gave the potion a wary glance, then turned to the merchant, his brow furrowed in suspicion. "Interesting? You're not gonna tell us it's magic moon juice, are you?"

The merchant chuckled. "Perhaps... but you'll have to figure that out yourselves."

With a final wink, the merchant tipped his hat, mounted his trusty steed, and began to ride off into the distance, disappearing into the shadows of the tunnel.

Po placed the blue potion carefully in his bag, shaking his head in amusement. "I'll never understand that guy."

Zap stretched and let out a dramatic yawn. "Well, at least we have a new mystery potion in our collection now. I just hope we don't end up drinking it by accident."

Po chuckled, shaking his head, as they continued down the tunnel, their footsteps echoing off the stone walls. The passage started to narrow, forcing them to walk in single file. The further they went, the more the walls seemed to close in, until they were nearly brushing their shoulders against the cool, damp stone.

"This place is getting tighter than my old school locker," Zap muttered, glancing around nervously.

Po stayed quiet, focused on the path ahead, but the tunnel soon became so cramped that they had to crawl. Eventually, the tunnel opened up just a little, leading to a small hole at the end, no wider than a large dog door. Through the gap, Po and Zap could see a small room on the other side.

"What's that?" Zap whispered.

Po peered through the opening. The room had three stone walls, dark and foreboding, with a fourth wall made entirely of iron bars. A barred gate sat in the middle of the wall, locked tight. In the corner of the room, sitting against the stone, was a small figure—a gnome-like being with a scraggly beard, hunched over and sobbing quietly to himself.

"He looks upset," Po whispered. "We should see if he needs help."

Zap nodded, and without hesitation, climbed easily through the opening, landing on the other side with a soft thud.

Po, however, wasn't as nimble. He squeezed his shoulders into the gap, grunting as he wriggled through. "I really need to stop eating so much bread..." he muttered under his breath, his face turning red with effort. After a struggle, he managed to pop out the other side, falling to the floor in an awkward heap

The sound startled the small, bearded figure. The gnome-like being jerked his head up, his eyes wide with alarm. "Wh-who's there?" he stammered, his voice shaky. "Stay back! I don't want any more trouble!"

Zap padded over, holding out his paws in a reassuring gesture. "Easy there, buddy. We're not here to hurt you."

The gnome-like figure's eyes darted to the wall behind them, and for the first time, Po and Zap got a good look at him. He was small, barely up to Po's waist, with a long grey beard and a dirty leather apron. His skin was weathered, and his eyes were red from crying.

Po approached slowly, his tone gentle. "Hey, we don't mean any harm. My name's Po, and this is Zap." He gestured to the dog, who wagged his tail and offered a friendly nod.

The small being sniffled, wiping his nose with the back of his hand. "I'm... I'm Braff. Braff the Blacksmith."

Zap tilted his head. "Blacksmith? What's that?"

Braff looked confused for a moment, then frowned. "You don't know what a blacksmith is? I make weapons and armour!"

Po's eyes lit up with interest. "You make weapons? That's pretty cool. But... why are you here, Braff? What happened?"

Braff's face darkened, and his shoulders slumped. "I... I was the Royal Blacksmith," he explained, his voice barely above a whisper. "I made weapons and armour for Princess Candy's guards. Then one day, a squad of Shadow Legion, led by the younger of the Shadow Twins, stormed the palace. They captured the princess... and threw me into this cell."

Zap's expression turned from curiosity to a flash of anger. "You did your duty, and they threw you in here for it? That's just wrong."

Po's heart sank as he listened, feeling sorry for the small blacksmith. "How long have you been here?"

Braff shook his head. "I'm not entirely sure. Could be days... or even weeks. Time moves strangely in this place."

Zap, ever practical, pointed at the small hole in the wall. "Why didn't you just go through the hole we came in through?"

Braff blinked at him, then glanced over to where the hole was. "What hole?"

Po and Zap spun around to find that the opening they had just crawled through had disappeared. In its place was nothing but solid, unbroken stone.

"Wha—?" Po stared at the wall in disbelief.

Zap growled. "Oh, that's just perfect."

Po, feeling a strange chill run down his spine, muttered, "It's like this place wants to keep us trapped."

Trying to keep his optimism, Po scratched his head. "It's probably protected by some kind of magic. A one-way passage."

Zap groaned. "Of course it is. So, what now?"

Po sighed, leaning against the wall. "I don't know... maybe someone will come by soon to let us out."

But hours dragged on, and no one came. They remained trapped in the cell with Braff, the iron bars still holding them firmly inside. The air was damp and cool, and Po found himself growing restless.

Zap, on the other hand, had been frantically running around the small space, pawing at the bars, growling, and even trying to bite them. "I swear, these bars are indestructible!" he muttered, backing away and shaking his head.

Braff had returned to his corner, muttering to himself in a low voice, occasionally glancing at the barred gate.

Po, ever the problem solver, sat down and began to think. He tried playing the flute, hoping its magic might work again. But this time, there was no hum, no glow—only silence. The magic of the flute had abandoned them.

As more time went by, Po opened his backpack to inspect what they had left. Inside, there were a few scattered items: his school Science book, a couple of blunted pencils, the dragon tooth, and the blue potion they'd gotten from the merchant.

Braff, noticing the potion, raised an eyebrow. "What's that?"

Po held up the vial. "I don't know. It's some kind of potion... but we don't know what it does."

Zap, who had been slumped against the bars, suddenly perked up. "Well, we've gotta try something, right? Maybe it'll make you super strong, and you can just smash our way out!"

Po stared at the blue liquid swirling inside the vial. "I'm not sure..."

Zap, grinning now, started throwing out ideas. "Or what if it makes you super small, and you can just walk through the gaps in the bars?"

Braff, catching on to the idea, added with a chuckle, "Or maybe it'll turn you into a key, and we can use you to unlock the door!"

Zap barked in agreement. "Exactly! It's worth a shot, right?"

Po looked from Braff to Zap, feeling their encouragement. A flicker of doubt stirred in him—this was a random potion from the merchant. What if it was dangerous? But as his gaze shifted to Braff's weary face, a resolve settled in him. They had to try something.

Slowly, he reached for the potion, flipping the lid open.

He stared at the blue liquid for a moment, then took a deep breath. "Here goes nothing."

8

VIII. The Shadow Tower

Po took a large gulp of the potion. Immediately, a strange sensation spread through his body—his skin tingled, his muscles tightened, and a strange warmth bubbled up inside him. He looked down at his hands, watching in disbelief as his skin darkened, turning a deep shadowy grey. His fingers elongated, and his nails sharpened into claws. He could feel himself growing taller, his limbs becoming stronger, and his clothes shifting into the black armour of a Shadow Guard. His entire body felt foreign.

"Po?" Zap whispered cautiously. Po opened his mouth to reply, but the sound that came out wasn't his voice at all. It was deep, like the rumble of thunder. "I... I think it worked," Po said, surprised at how menacing he sounded. But beneath the new exterior, Po's fear flickered—this disguise, though powerful, felt wrong, as though shadows were slipping into his soul.

Zap and Braff, both wide-eyed, took a step back. Braff's hands flew to his face. "Ah! What—what happened to you?" he screeched. Zap's ears shot up, and he yelped, jumping behind Braff. "Whoa! You're—Po, you're one of them!"

Po raised his clawed hand to touch his face, feeling the unfamiliar roughness of his shadowy skin. His voice was still deep and growly. "I... I know. It's just me, guys. No need to freak out." Despite his words, Po's heart beat faster. The pressure of his mission and the growing uncertainty of his true strength tightened around him like a chain.

But before they could settle their nerves, a voice called out from the hall, sharp and authoritative. "What's going on in there?"

Po stiffened. Heavy footsteps echoed down the stone corridor as another Shadow Guard approached. He had clearly heard the commotion.

Zap whispered, "Uh-oh..."

The guard appeared at the barred gate, his eyes narrowing as he spotted Po inside the cell. "What are you doing locked in there?" he growled, his gaze flicking between Po, Braff, and Zap.

Thinking quickly, Po stepped forward, trying to sound as official as possible. "I... uh... misplaced my key." His voice sounded more confident than he felt. "...and the lock jammed."

The guard blinked, raising a suspicious eyebrow. "Misplaced your key? A guard of the Shadow Legion? Incompetent much?"

Po swallowed nervously, trying to hold his ground. "It happens," he said, his deep voice steady. "Could you... let me out?

The guard eyed him warily, his gaze lingering on Zap and Braff, who were both standing very still, trying not to draw attention.

After a tense pause, the guard huffed and pulled out a keyring. "Fine. But this better not happen again, or I'll report you."

Po exhaled in relief as the guard unlocked the gate and swung it open. Po stepped out, his shadowy form looming over the other guard. But just as the guard was about to lock the gate again, he paused, his brow furrowing with renewed suspicion.

"Wait a second..." the guard muttered, turning back to Po. "Why were you down here in the first place? And where's your weapon?"

Po's heart raced. He fumbled for a response, but nothing came to mind. The guard's eyes darkened with suspicion, and his hand hovered over his sword hilt.

Zap, seeing the tension rise, acted fast. Before Po could react, Zap snatched the dragon tooth from the backpack that had been left inside the cell. With the heavy tooth clutched between his jaws, Zap leaped through the gate, his paws light and swift.

Without warning, Zap jumped up, swinging the dragon tooth in his mouth, and smacked the unsuspecting guard on the back of the head. The guard's eyes went wide in surprise before he collapsed to the ground, knocked out cold.

Po stared in disbelief, the relief quickly followed by a surge of self-doubt. How much longer could he protect everyone—and how much of the Shadow Tower's strength lay ahead?

Po stared in disbelief, while Braff gasped. "By the forge, what was that?"

Zap dropped the tooth and sat back on his haunches, looking rather pleased with himself. "Hey, we didn't have time to wait for you to bluff your way through that!"

Po let out a relieved laugh. "Nice one, Zap. I wasn't sure how much longer I could keep that up."

Braff, still wide-eyed, took a deep breath. "Well, I'll be! That was close."

Zap pawed at the dragon tooth, nudging it toward Braff. "So, Braff, any chance you could make something useful out of this?"

Braff's eyes lit up as he examined the dragon tooth. "Oh, yes... I've never seen such fine material. This could be turned into a magnificent weapon or armour."

Zap grinned. "We're thinking... a shield might come in handy."

Braff nodded thoughtfully, stroking his beard. "A shield. Yes, that could work. But I must warn you—I can only forge things quickly because of my limited magic. I'll need to concentrate."

Po watched as Braff knelt beside the dragon tooth, his hands hovering over it as he began to mutter a low, ancient chant. The air around them seemed to hum with energy as the blacksmith's eyes glowed faintly, his voice deep and rhythmic. He placed both hands on the tooth, and the room was filled with a soft, golden light.

The tooth shrank and shifted, its surface smoothing out as it morphed into the shape of a shield. Braff's muttering grew faster, his hands moving in careful patterns over the forming shield, as though he were moulding it out of clay. When the transformation was nearly complete, Braff's voice became a roar, and with one final motion, the shield solidified in his hands.

It gleamed with a faint, draconic sheen—dark, yet shimmering with hidden power. The surface was smooth, almost reflective, and faint wisps of energy curled around its edges, waiting to be unleashed.

Braff handed the shield to Po, who took it cautiously. "It's imbued with the spirit of the dragon," Braff explained, his eyes gleaming with pride. "It can absorb shadow magic."

"And it's super shiny too!" Zap exclaimed excitedly.

Po turned the shield over in his hands, feeling the weight of it. "This... is incredible."

Po strapped the shield to his arm, his heart racing with new hope.

The air inside the Shadow Towers was colder than Po had imagined, the thick stone walls absorbing every sound, every breath. His feet felt heavier as they ascended the narrow stairs, winding upward with only the dim light of torches flickering on the walls. The weight of the dragon-tooth shield strapped to his arm gave him strength, but the real challenge lay in blending in. His heart pounded beneath the black armour he wore—the transformation had been startling, even to him.

"I still can't get used to seeing you like that," Zap whispered from behind. His tone was light, but Po could hear the tension in his voice.

Braff trailed behind them, his footsteps quieter than Po expected from someone who spent his life hammering metal. "He's right, Po. You've got the look of a Shadow Guard, but I swear if you speak, you'll spook every creature in this place."

Po chuckled, his deep, rumbly voice still catching him off guard. "Let's just hope no one asks me too many questions."

But questions were inevitable. As they rounded another corner, a pair of guards stood blocking the path, their eyes narrowing at Po's approach. One of them stepped forward, eyeing him suspiciously.

"What are you doing here?" the guard demanded. "You're supposed to be on patrol, not wandering the tower."

Po swallowed nervously, trying to keep his posture strong. "I... was just doing a final sweep of the lower levels. Lost my bearings." His voice rumbled deep in his throat, but inside, he was shaking.

The guard crossed his arms. "Lost your bearings? In your own tower?"

Po, keeping his face steady, gave a small nod. "It happens sometimes, in this maze of a place." He forced a deep, menacing tone to keep up the ruse. "Is that going to be a problem?"

The guard raised an eyebrow but stepped aside.

As they climbed higher, they reached a large set of iron doors that led to a wide chamber. Po froze as they passed by, his eyes drawn to the rows of small cages inside the room, where various creatures—tiny, pure beings of the land—were trapped, their soft cries and moans echoing through the stone walls.

Po's heart twisted at the sight. His grip on the shield tightened. "We have to help them," he whispered, taking a step toward the chamber.

But Zap quickly darted in front of him, blocking his path. "Po, no! Look at all the guards in there. We can't risk it!"

Po clenched his fists. "But look at them. They're... they don't deserve this."

Zap's ears flattened against his head. "I know, Po. I know. But if we get caught, we won't be able to save anyone."

Braff gave a quiet grunt. "Zap's right. There's a time to fight and a time to be smart. Let's get out of here while we still can."

Reluctantly, Po turned away from the sight, his chest heavy with guilt. They continued to ascend the tower in silence, the only sound being their echoing footsteps.

The air grew colder as they neared the top of the tower, the stone stairs winding ever higher. Po could feel his skin tingling—something was wrong.

"I... I think the potion's wearing off," Po muttered, glancing down at his hands.

His fingers were slowly returning to their normal colour, patches of his skin flickering between the shadowy grey and his usual pale hue. He felt himself shrinking, his legs shortening, his voice no longer carrying the same deep, ominous tone.

Braff, glancing upward, pointed to the narrowing spiral stairs above them. "We're almost there. One of the Shadow Twins resides at the top of this tower—be careful, Po."

Po's heart pounded harder. His hands, now half-shaded and half-normal, trembled as they gripped the dragon-tooth shield.

He could feel the last remnants of the potion slipping away, his voice losing its deep resonance. He exchanged a nervous look with Zap, who gave him a lopsided grin to calm him.

Finally, they reached the top, and in front of them was a large, arched wooden door, the carvings on its surface dark and swirling with shadow-like patterns. Po hesitated for a moment before slowly pushing the door open.

Po felt his breath hitch as they stepped into the large chamber at the top of the tower. The room was dim, its walls draped in shadows that flickered and shifted like they were alive. At the centre stood an antique desk, covered in a sprawling map of the kingdom, intricate and marked in several places. Leaning over it was a tall figure, his back turned to them—Tezcat, the younger of the Shadow Twins.

Tezcat didn't seem to notice them at first, his fingers tracing a line across the map, his posture calm and composed, as if he were lost in thought. Po's heart pounded in his chest, his grip tightened on his sword and shield.

Zap leaned toward Po, whispering, "So, uh... do we just sneak up behind him, or—"

Before Zap could finish, Tezcat's voice cut through the silence, smooth and sharp, like glass. "Impressive," he said, without looking up. His voice was calm, but beneath it was a dangerous edge. "I was wondering when you'd finally show yourselves."

Po froze, a chill running down his spine. Tezcat turned slowly, his eyes like cold steel, glinting in the dim light. His skin was pale, almost translucent, his features angular and sharp. Shadows clung to him like a second skin, curling around his form as if he were one with the darkness.

"I'm surprised you made it this far," Tezcat said softly, his lips barely curling into what could have been a smile—or a sneer. "I had expected the witch or the dragon to finish you off. And yet, here you stand."

Po swallowed hard, feeling the tension rise in the room. "We're here for Princess Candy," he said, his voice more confident than he felt. "and stop you and your brother's evil plans!"

Tezcat's smile deepened, but there was no warmth in it—only cold amusement. "Stop us?" He glanced down at the map before him, tapping a finger on one of the marked locations. "You have no idea what wheels are already in motion."

Zap stepped forward, his ears pinned back, growling. "How about we kick your shadowy butt?"

Tezcat's eyes flicked over to Zap, the barest hint of amusement in his gaze. "Ah, the brave little companion," he said softly, almost mockingly. "Always so eager to bite at the ankles of giants."

Po shot a glance at Zap, warning him to stay calm, then turned back to Tezcat. "We're here to free the princess, and we're not leaving without her."

Tezcat let out a low chuckle, stepping away from the desk, his hands clasped behind his back as he circled them slowly. His movements were measured, deliberate, like a predator toying with its prey.

"I see you're still holding onto hope," he mused, his voice a soft murmur. "Hope is such a fragile thing. It crumbles so easily... just like sand." His gaze settled on Po, his eyes narrowing. "And yet, you persist. Why?"

Po felt a knot tighten in his stomach. He wasn't sure how to answer. Why did they keep pushing forward, despite the odds? Was it simply to save Princess Candy? Or was it something deeper?

Tezcat's eyes began to turn pale, drained of colour, as though the shadows themselves were controlling him. His expression darkened as he raised a hand. The shadows in the room shifted, swirling around him like a living thing. The shadows crawled across the walls like creeping vines. Tezcat's presence seemed to grow, his figure looming larger in the dim light.

"There's a reason I'm here," Tezcat said, his voice soft but dangerous. "You're not the first to come for her. And you won't be the last. But you... you've piqued my interest." He took another step closer, his gaze never leaving Po's. "Tell me, Po... what will you do when hope isn't enough?"

With another flick of Tezcat's hand, the shadows on the walls surged forward, forming into creatures—dark, swirling figures with glowing eyes and indistinct, monstrous forms. They moved silently but menacingly toward Po and his companions.

The shadow creatures lunged forward. Instinctively, Po raised the dragon-tooth shield, and the moment the first creature hit it, a surge of dark energy flowed into the shield, absorbed into its smooth, shimmering surface. Po gasped as the shield began to hum with power, faint wisps of shadow swirling around its edges.

He glanced at Zap and Braff. "The shield... it's absorbing their magic!"

Zap's ears perked up. "Well, that's handy!"

Another creature lunged, but Po was ready this time. He deflected the attack with the shield, the magic once again absorbed. The shield glowed faintly now, buzzing with the shadow magic stored within.

But with each hit, Po's arm trembled—absorbing Tezcat's magic wasn't just draining the creatures, it was draining him.

Tezcat's calm tone belied the menace in his words. "You think you've mastered the shadows? You're merely toying with embers, while I command the inferno."

With a graceful motion, Tezcat raised both hands, and the shadows in the room surged. The air grew cold, and the shadows on the walls began to writhe and shift, forming tendrils that lashed toward Po. This time, it wasn't just the creatures—Tezcat was commanding the shadows themselves.

Po braced himself, but the tendrils slammed into the shield with crushing force, nearly sending him to his knees. His chest tightened as his own energy drained faster than the shield absorbed it.

He glanced at Zap and Braff, a flicker of desperation in his gaze. "This shield—it's powerful, but I don't know how much more it can take."

Braff took a step forward, his eyes narrowing in determination. "Then let me help." With a grunt, he pulled a small, glowing hammer from his belt—a simple blacksmith's tool, but imbued with a faint, magical light. "It's not much, but it'll buy us some time."

Braff slammed the hammer down on the stone floor, and a wave of light rippled outward, forming a barrier that pushed back the encroaching shadows. The creatures hissed, recoiling from the light as it temporarily held them at bay.

Tezcat tilted his head slightly, watching Braff's barrier with mild curiosity. "Interesting. A blacksmith with magic... Rare, but ultimately useless." His voice was calm, but there was a growing edge of frustration behind it.

The barrier wavered as the shadows pressed harder, testing its strength. Braff grunted, sweat beading on his forehead. "I can't hold this forever!"

Po's mind raced. He had the power of the dragon shield, but Tezcat's command of the shadows was overwhelming. They needed a way to turn the tide. "Zap!" Po called out. "We need a distraction!"

Zap's eyes darted around the room before locking onto the map on Tezcat's desk. A mischievous grin spread across his face. "Gotcha buddy."

While Po and Braff held the line, Zap darted around the shadow creatures, his small form slipping through the chaos unnoticed. He bounded up onto the desk, his paws landing with a soft thud next to the map. Tezcat's eyes snapped to him, but Zap was too quick.

Zap leaped onto the desk, knocking over one of the glowing orbs that lit the room. It shattered on the ground with a bright flash, and the sudden light disoriented the shadow creatures, causing them to shrink back momentarily.

Tezcat growled, his calm demeanour cracking. "Bad do—"

Before he could finish, Po saw his chance. He raised the dragon-tooth shield, now glowing brightly with the stored shadow magic, and charged toward Tezcat. The shield buzzed in his hands, crackling with energy.

Tezcat spun around, catching sight of Po charging at him. The surprise flickered in his widened eyes, a rare crack in his usual composure. With a fierce determination, Po thrust the shield forward. The energy stored within it exploded in a dazzling burst of light, blinding Tezcat and further illuminating the room.

The magic crashed into Tezcat, sending him stumbling back. For the first time, Tezcat's calm composure slipped. He raised his hands, trying to deflect the blast, but the energy surged around him, swirling like a storm. His form flickered, the shadows struggling to hold together.

Tezcat pushed back, his eyes blazing with fury. "You... dare..." Tezcat growled, his voice strained but seething with anger.

Braff, still straining to hold the barrier, shouted, "Po! Now! Hit him again!"

Po didn't hesitate. With all his strength, he swung the shield again, channelling the last of the shadow magic. The energy collided with Tezcat in a brilliant flash of light and shadow, and this time, the Shadow Twin was thrown back, crashing against the wall.

The shadows around him flickered, and for the first time, Tezcat looked genuinely surprised, his breath laboured. His cold, calculating eyes locked on Po, and for a moment, there was silence.

Then, with a low, dangerous growl, Tezcat's form began to dissolve into the shadows themselves. His voice echoed through the chamber, cold and sharp. "This is far from over."

The oppressive darkness in the room began to lift, and the remaining shadow creatures dissolved into nothingness. The chamber was quiet, the tension slowly ebbing away.

Po lowered the dragon shield, his hands shaking from the effort. He felt exhausted, but there was a sense of victory, however brief it might be.

Zap bounded over, his tail wagging furiously. "Ha! Did you see that? I guess he wasn't too bright after all!"

Po, still catching his breath, looked at the spot where Tezcat had vanished. "He'll be back," he muttered, his voice filled with determination. "We'll need to be ready for whatever comes next."

Zap, ever the optimist, hopped up onto the desk. "Yeah, yeah, but for now... we're alive, and we've got this super shiny shield. I call that a win!"

Braff chuckled softly, nodding in agreement. "Aye, and we've got something else." He gestured to the map on the desk. "That thing Tezcat was so focused on—it seemed important. We'd best take a look."

Po walked over to the desk, his eyes scanning the marked locations on the map. There was a lot they didn't yet understand, but one thing was clear: this wasn't over. Not by a long shot.

9

IX. Podkin & Ham's Light Factory

The room was quiet, except for the faint hum of tension that still lingered after the battle. Po stood in front of the large, worn map, tracing his fingers along the marked locations scattered across the kingdom. His brow furrowed as he studied the thin lines that connected some of the red-marked spots.

"This looks like more than just a map," Po murmured, his eyes following the network of lines. "These locations... they're scattered everywhere. And these lines—they're connecting only a few places."

Zap peeked over his shoulder, squinting at the map as though trying to make sense of it. "Looks like someone's playing connect-the-dots," he muttered, "but with evil towers and creepy locations."

Braff, standing nearby, rubbed his chin thoughtfully. "Or perhaps these are key places of power, where the Shadow Twins are concentrating their influence. These lines might be their way of controlling the kingdom."

Po nodded, his gaze returning to the largest marking on the map—the Shadow Tower, where they now stood. "But why are only some places connected? What are they trying to control?"

After a moment of silence, Braff gestured toward the room around them. "There's bound to be more than just this map. The Shadow Twins don't leave their plans out in the open. If Tezcat's marked these places, there's something specific they're after. We should search the room, see if we can find anything else that might explain Tezcat's plans."

Zap stretched, a sly grin spreading across his face. "I work better when I'm moving. Time for a little dance party."

♫ Beat that Shadow guy,
coz' we refused to yield,
he fled with a cry,
Coz Po gave 'em a piece of his shield ♫

With that, Zap began to hum and spin in circles, his tail wagging as he danced around the room. Po and Braff, on the other hand, searched the room more methodically, opening drawers and inspecting bookshelves for any hidden clues. Zap's carefree attitude seemed infectious, even though Po remained focused.

Just as Po bent down to inspect an old, dusty tome, he heard a thud followed by a surprised yelp. He looked up to see Zap on the ground, tangled in a heavy cloth that had been hanging from the far wall. The cloth had fallen, revealing something behind it.

It was an ornate mirror, large and framed with intricate carvings of swirling vines, fantastical creatures, and strange symbols. Dust covered its surface, but even through the grime, Po could tell it was ancient and powerful.

Po's breath caught in his throat as he knelt in front of it, his fingers grazing the edge of the mirror. It reminded him of the mirror from Portadale, the one they had stepped through to enter this strange world. He gently wiped away some of the dust, revealing the glass beneath.

The moment Po touched the mirror's surface, it began to swirl to life. The air around them grew heavier, a faint crackling energy seeming to emanate from the mirror as if something powerful was waiting on the other side. Colours danced and shimmered within the glass, creating a mesmerizing, swirling light.

Zap, still recovering from his fall, peeked up from behind Po, his eyes wide. "Oh, great. Another magical portal. Should we step through it, or maybe... run away?"

Braff eyed the glowing mirror, his hand resting on the hilt of his hammer. "A portal... but where does it lead?"

Po hesitated, standing back up and turning toward the map again. He scanned the locations once more, looking for any clue as to where the mirror might take them. His eyes landed on the Shadow Tower, marked clearly at the centre, and then followed the thin line connecting it to another point labelled "Podkin & Ham's Light Factory."

Po squinted at the name, intrigued. " Podkin & Ham?"

At the mention of the name, Braff's eyes widened with recognition.

Braff took a step closer, his voice suddenly filled with awe. "Podkin & Ham? I've heard of them! They're one of the most famous lamp makers in the kingdom."

Po and Zap exchanged glances before speaking in unison. "Famous?"

Braff's expression softened, and he began to explain with a touch of reverence in his voice.

"Podkin & Ham have been around for centuries, crafting the finest lamps and lanterns the kingdom has ever seen. They're not just ordinary lights—they shine brighter, last longer, and some are even said to possess magical properties."

Po noticed a flicker of nostalgia in Braff's eyes ad he continued. "People from all over seek them out, hoping to get their hands on a Podkin & Ham creation. But the secret behind their lights has

always been kept under lock and key, guarded as fiercely as the kingdom's treasures."

Zap grinned. "So, a factory full of magical glowing lights? Whose bright idea was that?"

Po chuckled but couldn't help feeling thoughtful. He pointed at the map again. "If this mirror connects to their factory, Tezcat must have some reason for linking it to the tower. What does he want from there?"

Braff's brows furrowed. "Whatever it is, it can't be good."

The mirror's swirling colours grew brighter, casting a soft glow around the room. The hum coming from it seemed to grow louder, as though beckoning them to step through. Po, Zap, and Braff exchanged nervous glances before turning back to the glowing portal.

Braff gripped the handle of his hammer, his voice a little shaky. "Are we sure this is the way to go?"

Zap, always the bold one, smirked and stepped forward. "Well, glowing magical portals don't show up every day. Let's go before we miss the show."

The glowing light enveloped the trio as they passed through the mirror.

As they stepped out of the other side, they emerged into a large, dimly lit room. The first thing they noticed was the cold air, heavy with dust and an unsettling stillness. In front of them stretched a vast factory floor, but something felt terribly wrong. The air crack-led with a strange, residual energy, as if the factory walls were holding onto echoes of powerful magic that once flowed through them.

Rows of once-great machinery stood in disrepair, bent and bro-ken, as though they had been deliberately sabotaged. Glass shards littered the floor, glinting faintly in the weak glow of the few

surviving lamps that hung crookedly from the walls. There were deep gashes in the metal equipment, as if someone had taken great pleasure in tearing it apart. The air smelled of burnt metal and magic.

Po took a cautious step forward, crunching broken glass be-neath his feet. His eyes scanned the room, taking in the destruc-tion. "What happened here?"

Braff didn't answer. He was already walking slowly ahead of them, his eyes wide as he surveyed the wreckage. His once sure and confident expression had crumbled. Podkin & Ham's Light Fac-tory—a beacon of the kingdom's pride—was in ruins.

Kneeling, Braff picked up a shattered piece of a lantern, his hand trembling as he turned it over. His usually strong voice was thick with emotion. "This... this place was the pride of the king-dom." He looked around, his eyes darkening. "A symbol of light, of hope. And now..."

He paused, the light catching on a faintly engraved name at the base of the lantern. "My father used to bring me here when I was a boy. Podkin & Ham's lights—they meant more to the people than you could ever know. I grew up dreaming of making something so pure, so lasting..." His voice trailed off, choked by grief.

As Braff clenched his fists, the shards of the lantern slipped from his hands and fell back onto the floor.

Po knelt beside him, placing a comforting hand on Braff's shoulder. "I'm really sorry, Braff. This place must have meant everything to the people who worked here... to you."

Braff nodded, his gaze fixed on the broken lantern. "It's more than just a factory. This was a place of magic and craftsmanship, where every lantern that left these walls carried a piece of light into the darkest parts of the kingdom. To see it reduced to this... It's like losing a piece of myself."

They stood in silence for a moment, the weight of the destruction sinking in.

Zap, always quick to cut the tension, stepped forward, gingerly avoiding the glass beneath his paws. "Well, if they were going for a 'broken glass chic,' I'd say they've really nailed it." He grinned. "Or should I say... smashed it?"

Po shot him a look, his lips twitching with amusement despite the mood. "Zap..."

Zap shrugged. "Hey, I'm just saying, whoever did this had a real knack for interior destruction."

Determined to find out what had happened, Po, Zap, and Braff began to search the factory floor. They moved through the wreckage carefully, stepping over toppled machinery and broken pieces of lanterns. Po couldn't shake the uneasy feeling gnawing at him; it was as if the factory itself was watching them. Occasionally, he'd catch a faint hum or whisper, a strange resonance echoing in the shards of glass scattered across the floor.

The lamps on the walls flickered weakly, their once strong and magical light now dim and irregular. One of the lamps suddenly sputtered and went out, casting a deeper shadow across the room. Po stopped, his hand instinctively reaching for his sword as he looked around, feeling the prickling sense of being watched.

Braff inspected the damage closely, his experienced eye taking in the details. "This wasn't done by accident. They were looking for something."

Po, still running his fingers over the shattered machinery, frowned. "Why tear it all apart like this? If the lamps were so valuable, why not just steal them?"

Braff shook his head, kneeling beside another smashed lantern. "They weren't looking for the lamps themselves. They were looking for the source of the magic that powers them."

Zap's ears perked up, curiosity flashing in his eyes. "The source? You mean like the secret behind why Podkin & Ham's lights are so special?"

Braff nodded. "Yes. Every lantern created here is imbued with magic. But the magic doesn't come from the lanterns themselves—it comes from a hidden source. That's what makes them brighter, stronger, and more powerful than any other lights in the kingdom. And that's what the Shadow Twins were after."

Zap's eyes flickered with a mix of fear and fascination. "So, wait... if the magic source is here somewhere, does that mean whatever's left of it might still be... active?" His gaze shifted nervously, as if expecting the factory's shadows to come alive at any moment.

They continued searching the factory, moving deeper into the wreckage. As they passed by a large, overturned table, Po's eyes landed on symbols scratched into the metal near the broken machinery—dark, jagged markings that looked unnatural, as though carved by something inhuman.

Po squinted at the symbols, his heart sinking. "These marks... they're the same ones I saw at the Shadow Tower."

Braff's face darkened as he approached the symbols, clenching his fists. "The Shadow Twins were here."

As they continued their search, they found what looked like a small office tucked into a corner of the factory. The door hung loosely on its hinges, and inside, the remains of papers and broken furniture were scattered across the floor. It looked like the place had been thoroughly ransacked.

Zap rifled through a drawer, pulling it open with a grunt, only to find it completely empty. "Well, this must be where they keep all the nothing!"

Po frowned as he looked around the room. "Where are Podkin and Ham? Do you think they were taken by the Shadow Twins?"

Braff shook his head firmly. "No. If the Shadow Twins had taken them, there would be more signs of a struggle. We would've found something. But there's no trace of them." He looked up, his eyes hard. "Which means they must've escaped."

Po nodded, thinking aloud. "Or maybe they're hiding. If they knew the Shadow Twins were after the source of their magic, they would've taken it with them."

Zap's ears perked up, his tail wagging slightly. "So, they're still out there, waiting for a hero to swoop in." He flashed a grin. "Guess that's our cue."

Po, Zap, and Braff made their way toward the exit, all deep in thought, though for varying reasons. The silence was broken only by the occasional creak of broken machinery and the crunch of glass underfoot.

As they neared the large, rusted doors, Po noticed a faint, eerie glow starting to gather in the corners of the factory, flickering like a dying ember reigniting. Strange whispers seemed to echo, barely audible but persistent, as if the broken machines themselves were trying to speak.

Zap's eyes gleamed mischievously. He spotted one of the last remaining intact glowing orbs hanging from a thin wire near the corner of the room, its soft light casting a gentle glow over the darkened factory.

Zap, grinning from ear to ear, nudged Po's side. "Hey, I think we deserve a little souvenir."

Po sighed, glancing over at the orb. "Just be careful, Zap."

But Zap wasn't listening. He was already making his way toward the light, his tail wagging with excitement. "Braff, give me a lift!"

Braff, amused but hesitant, bent down to let Zap clamber onto his broad shoulders. "Alright but be careful with that thing. It might be the only unbroken lamp left in here."

Zap, balancing on Braff's shoulders, stretched his paws toward the orb. He could just barely reach it, his claws scraping the delicate surface. "Almost... got it..." He gave the orb a gentle tap, and it swung lazily on its thin wire, moving out of his reach.

"Come on..." Zap grumbled, reaching further as the orb swung back toward him. "Just a little —"

At the exact moment Zap stretched his paws again, there was a sharp snap. The fragile string holding the orb gave way, and with wide eyes, Zap watched as the glowing orb plummeted toward the floor.

Po's heart sank. "Nooo..."

The orb hit the ground with a shattering crash, sending shards of glass scattering across the floor. For a split second, the entire factory lit up, an intense glow that surged through the room like a burst of sunlight breaking through storm clouds.

Then it was gone. The orb's light flickered out, leaving behind only pieces of shattered glass.

Zap hopped down from Braff's shoulders, rubbing his paws sheepishly. "Uh... oops. "

Braff sighed heavily, glancing at the shattered remains. "That was probably the last one..."

Zap shrugged, trying to lighten the mood. "Look, I'm pretty sure that one was a fake anyway. "

Po, trying to hide a grin, shook his head. "Well, I guess we should—"

Before Po could finish, an intense, cold breeze swept through the factory, as if all the air had been sucked toward a single point. A low, ominous hum filled the space, and the ground beneath their feet began to tremble. Tiny shards of glass and fragments of metal started to rise, suspended in mid-air, drawn by some invisible force.

Zap's ears twitched. "Uh... was that me? I don't think that was me."

The hum grew louder, and Po felt an electric prickling along his skin, a feeling that made his instincts scream to run. "This... this feels wrong," he muttered.

Suddenly, from the heaps of broken lamps and twisted metal, something began to stir. The shattered machinery rattled, gears grinding slowly to life. Fragments of glass lifted from the ground, suspended in mid-air. All around them, rusted tools, and gears began to tremble and shift.

"Uh, guys?" Zap said, taking a slow step back.

Po, Zap, and Braff stood frozen as the last sparks of magic from the shattered orb swirled together. The debris and fragments of glass lifted into the air, swirling faster and faster until they collided with a piece of twisted machinery in the corner. Slowly, the fragments and metal formed into a single, towering creature.

It was a hulking mass of jagged glass, sharp gears, and broken machinery parts. A glowing core of faint light pulsed in its chest, and its glassy limbs crackled with unstable energy as it moved. The sound of grinding metal and scraping glass filled the air as it took its first staggering steps toward them.

Zap's tail drooped, his eyes widening in disbelief. "I guess it wasn't a fake after all."

Braff gripped his hammer tightly, his eyes narrowed. "I don't like the look of that thing."

The creature lunged forward with surprising speed, swinging a jagged arm made of broken gears and sharp metal directly at Po. Po barely had time to raise his shield, deflecting the blow as sparks flew. The force of the impact sent him stumbling backward.

Po quickly steadied himself, his heart racing. "It's strong," he muttered, raising his sword. "I think we have to break its core!"

With a swift motion, Po slashed at the creature's glowing chest. His sword connected with the core, and for a moment, the creature seemed to disintegrate. The pieces of glass and metal collapsed onto the floor in a heap.

Zap blinked, his ears perking up. "Well, that was ea—"

Before he could finish, the pieces of the creature began to float again, pulling themselves back together. Within seconds, the creature had reformed, standing taller and more menacing than before.

"That... thing," Po murmured, staring at the glowing core. "It's using the broken machinery to pull itself back together."

The creature lunged again, its sharp limbs swinging dangerously close to Braff, who blocked the strike with his hammer, but the force sent him staggering backward. Po slashed at it once more, only for the creature to reform yet again.

"It just keeps coming back!" Po growled, frustration mounting. He struck the creature repeatedly, his sword slicing through its body and shattering its core, but no matter how many times it fell apart, it always reformed itself—stronger and faster than before.

"It's pulling energy from the factory!" Po realized, watching in horror as more broken pieces joined the creature. "If we don't stop it from drawing power, it'll just keep coming back."

Braff swung his hammer at one of the creature's legs, managing to send a shard of glass flying, but the creature responded with a swift, jagged strike. The blow caught Braff off-guard, slicing across his side and sending him sprawling onto the floor.

Zap gasped, rushing to Braff's side. "Braff! Are you okay?"

Braff, clutching his side, grimaced in pain. "I'm fine."

Po's eyes darted around the room, his mind racing. Every time they hit the creature, it reassembled itself. And now, with Braff injured, they were running out of options.

Zap dodged another swipe from the creature, his voice frantic. "Po, what should we do?!"

Po's chest tightened as he glanced at Braff, who was struggling to stand. His heart pounded with the weight of the decision. Braff needed help. But staying to fight would mean putting all their lives at risk.

The creature was relentless, and the truth was sinking in; they were overpowered. They couldn't win this fight, not this time.

"We have to leave! Now!" Po shouted, making the decision.

With Zap's help, Po grabbed Braff by the arm, pulling him to his feet. Together, they staggered toward the factory's exit, the sound of grinding metal and crackling energy growing louder behind them as the creature closed in.

Zap darted ahead, reaching the doors first. "Come on, Po! Hurry!"

They pushed through the large, rusted doors, stumbling outside just as the creature lunged at them. Po slammed the door shut behind them, the sound of the creature crashing into it reverberating through the factory.

For a tense moment, they stood there, hearts pounding, listening to the muffled sounds of the creature battering against the other side. But the door held.

Zap let out a breath he didn't realize he was holding. "Well... guess it doesn't know how to open doors."

Po turned to Braff, who was leaning heavily against the wall, clutching his side. Po's heart sank when he saw the blood seeping through Braff's fingers.

"Braff..." Po's voice was thick with concern. "You're bleeding."

Braff, breathing heavily, managed a weak smile. "Aye... it's a deep one, but I'll be fine. " His voice wavered, though he tried to sound strong. "You've got more important things to worry about. That thing in there... it's not stopping. And there's still a princess to save."

Po shook his head, his voice soft but firm. "We're not leaving you behind."

Braff gave a small chuckle, though it was strained with pain. "You'll have to, Po. You have a mission. And I've done my part." He winced as the pain surged through him, but he kept his gaze steady on Po. "Go now. Find the Princess. Defeat the Shadow Twins."

Zap, usually full of jokes, was quiet for once. His eyes darted between Po and Braff, his tail low. "But... Braff, we can't—"

Braff placed a heavy hand on Zap's head, ruffling his fur gently. "I've been around a long time. I'll manage. You two—" he paused, his voice cracking slightly, "you two have bigger things to worry about than an old blacksmith."

Braff then leaned back against the factory wall, his hand still pressed against his wound. "There's a path you can take that's not far from here. From there, there will be a river. Follow it, and you'll reach the Princess Candy's Castle. I heard that's where she is being held."

For a moment, the only sound was the faint rustling of the wind and the distant creaks from within the factory.

Po knelt beside Braff, his voice hoarse. "I don't know how to thank you. For everything."

Zap nudged Po gently, his voice quieter than usual. "We'll come back for you, Braff. After we save the Princess, we'll come back."

With one final glance back, Po and Zap turned and began walking down the path Braff had pointed out, their footsteps heavy with both determination and sorrow.

As they disappeared into the distance, Braff leaned his head back against the factory wall, closing his eyes. His breathing slowed, but a soft smile remained on his lips.

X. Sleeping on the Job

Po and Zap walked along the winding path. The silence between them felt weighty, punctuated only by the soft crunch of dirt beneath their boots and the occasional rustling of leaves.

As they walked further, Po noticed something familiar—a cluster of three large, ancient trees standing close together, their gnarled branches intertwined like old friends sharing whispered secrets. The trees looked exactly like the ones they had encountered earlier in their journey. Po blinked in confusion, and Zap quickly picked up on it too.

Zap frowned, his tail flicking as he stared up at the towering trees. "Wait a second. Aren't those the same trees we saw near Wilkwood? What are they doing all the way out here?"

Po tilted his head, studying them. "It... it looks like them. But how could they—?

Zap cut him off. "They probably flew here. I mean c'mon, somethings gotta fly in this place."

Before they could puzzle it out further, the wise tree stirred, its deep voice rumbling like thunder across the clearing. "Ah, young travellers, you seem surprised. But the world is full of surprises, is it not? Do not take everything at face value. In life, things often move when we believe them to be still. Even trees, when they have reason."

Po raised his eyebrows, glancing at Zap.

Zap snorted. "What's next? Dancing mountains?"

The pessimistic tree groaned, its long branches swaying like they were too heavy to bear. "Surprises? Ha! All surprises lead to is disappointment. Just look at the Podkin & Ham lamps—once brilliant, now shattered, like everything in life. Everything crumbles into dust in the end."

Zap raised an eyebrow and crossed his arms. "Wait, how do *you* know about the light factory? You've been standing here the whole time."

The wise tree smirked. "We have roots in many places. We see much more than you realize."

A chill crept up Po's spine at those words, a reminder of how interconnected everything in this world seemed to be. The trees weren't just witnesses—they were observers, silent guardians with knowledge he couldn't even begin to fathom.

Before Po could respond, the silly tree burst out in a fit of laughter, its leaves rustling like a hundred tambourines. "Break apart? Fall? What are we, pottery? Lighten up, branch-breath! These two are still standing, aren't they? Ha! Imagine if they turned into squirrels! Running from trouble with their little squirrel tails wagging behind them! Just imagine Po with nuts for lunch and Zap digging for acorns! Hah!"

Zap grinned, unable to help himself. "I mean... I *would* make a great squirrel."

Po shook his head, chuckling softly. "You're already enough trouble without turning into a squirrel."

As they moved past the trees, their strange banter faded into the wind, leaving Po and Zap both amused and slightly unsettled. The trees' words—odd as they were—lingered in their minds as they continued toward the river.

The path opened up to a sparkling river, its surface shimmering under the golden sunlight. On the riverbank, a small, weathered boat bobbed gently, tethered to a moss-covered wooden post by a frayed rope.

The boat looked as old as time itself, its wood warped and cracked from years of wear. What little paint remained had peeled off in places, leaving it bare and rough. Moss clung to its sides, and inside, a pair of oars lay, the handles worn smooth from use.

Zap eyed the boat sceptically, his tail twitching with doubt. "Are we seriously going to get in that thing? It looks like it could sink just by the thought of water."

Po crouched down, inspecting the boat's rough edges. "It's definitely seen better days..."

"Better *centuries*," Zap muttered under his breath. "You really think it'll hold?"

Po gave him a small smile. "Well, it hasn't sunk yet, right? And it's our only way across."

Zap sighed dramatically, hopping into the boat and settling himself at the bow. "Fine, but if this thing starts taking on water, I'm swimming back to those wisecracking trees."

Po chuckled, giving the boat a push and hopping in. He grabbed the oars and began rowing, the boat gliding smoothly along the river's gentle current.

As they floated downstream, the river widened, and on the horizon, Princess Candy's castle loomed into view. Even from a distance, it was a sight to behold.

The castle shimmered with opalescent hues—pale pinks, violets, and soft blues—its walls made from an iridescent stone that glowed in the sunlight. Towers spiralled high into the sky, each crowned with delicate spires that glittered like diamonds. The structure was breathtaking, a dreamlike vision of beauty and magic, as if it had been crafted from stardust and moonlight.

Zap glanced back at Po, his expression unimpressed. "Still looks like someone's idea of a fancy birthday cake. All it's missing is the candles."

Po laughed softly. "You think they'll let us light it up when we get there?"

"Depends on if we make it there," Zap quipped, leaning back and letting the gentle current carry them closer.

As they continued, the landscape along the riverbank shifted. On one side of the river, vibrant, trumpet-shaped flowers swayed in the breeze. Their petals were a dazzling array of colours—every colour was present—all glowing faintly under the sunlight. As Po and Zap passed by, something unexpected happened: the flowers began to lift their blossoms toward the sky, and a soft, melodic hum filled the air.

Po blinked in surprise as each flower produced its own note, creating a harmonious, soothing serenade that echoed over the water. Together, they played a gentle melody that wrapped around them like a lullaby, the sound both peaceful and enchanting.

Zap's ears perked up, his eyes wide with wonder. "Whoa. I didn't know flowers could do *that*."

Po leaned forward, listening in awe. "Me neither. This place just keeps getting stranger."

The flowers continued their serenade, swaying gently as they passed. For a moment, the world felt calm and peaceful, the music lulling them into a sense of serenity.

But then, something caught Po's eye—a faint glow of white light shining from beyond the flowers, deeper into the trees. The light flickered, casting soft halos over the plants like a distant star beckoning them closer.

Po pointed toward the glow; his curiosity piqued. "Zap, do you see that light? What do you think it is?"

Before Zap could respond, a familiar whistle echoed across the water. A train whistle.

Both Po and Zap turned toward the opposite side of the river, where a train was slowly making its way along the tracks that followed the riverbank.

As the train drew closer, they saw a familiar figure leaning out of one of the windows—Habzar, the jolly leaf-haired creature they had met before. He grinned broadly, waving at them with both hands.

"Hey Zap, Hi Po!" Habzar called out, his voice booming over the train's rumble. "You've made it so far! Good luck with the princess!"

Zap stood up in the boat, waving back. "Hey, Habzar! Don't suppose you have any sausages aboard?"

Habzar chuckled, his eyes twinkling. "Sorry Zap, we're all out!"

The train's whistle blew once more as it chugged off into the distance, Habzar's wave disappearing as the train rolled further down the track.

"Well," Po said with a grin, "that was unexpected."

Zap shook his head, laughing. "Story of our lives."

As the train disappeared, the boat drifted further downstream, the melody of the flowers fading behind them. Soon, another dock came into view—larger and more well-maintained than the last one. The planks were smooth and dark, stretching out over the river, welcoming them to shore.

As the boat gently drifted toward the dock, Po and Zap noticed a figure pacing frantically near the end of the wooden platform. It was a dog—but not just any dog. He looked almost identical to Zap, with the same golden fur and alert posture. However, this dog sported a thick, bushy black moustache that curled at the ends. He wore a miner's helmet, complete with a tiny flickering torch, and a dusty brown vest over his rugged mining clothes.

Every few seconds, the dog muttered to himself, a constant stream of anxious commentary as he circled, occasionally stopping to scratch his head or pat his vest pockets as if hoping his missing pickaxe might magically reappear.

Po blinked, squinting at the miner. "Zap... is it just me, or does that dog look exactly like you?"

Zap whipped around, his ears flicking back in disbelief. "What? No way!" He gave the miner a long look, scowling as he took in the familiar features. "You've got to be kidding. We look *nothing* alike! Just because we're both dogs doesn't mean we all look the same, Po!"

Po chuckled but didn't push the matter further as they pulled up to the dock. The miner dog was still muttering to himself, oblivious to their arrival. His paws shifted through the dirt as he sniffed and searched the area with frantic urgency.

"Where did I put it? I could've sworn it was here..." the miner mumbled, his voice tinged with panic. "If it's gone again, they're gonna say I've cursed paws!"

"Hey there!" Po called out as he tied the boat to the dock. "You okay? What are you looking for?"

The miner's head snapped up, his eyes wide with panic. "Oh, thank goodness! I've lost my pickaxe again!" He trotted over to them, his thick moustache twitching nervously. "It's the fourth time this month! And if my supervisor finds out, I'll lose my job for sure!"

Zap raised an eyebrow, tilting his head. "Again? How do you keep losing something like a pickaxe?"

The miner dog sighed, his tail drooping. "I don't know! I got this little ritual—gotta pat my helmet twice and turn around before I start working. Always keeps my tools in place. Or... it used to!" He cast a suspicious glance over his shoulder. "I was mining the crystal rocks just up the hill, took a break for lunch, and when I woke up, it was gone!"

Zap smirked. "What did you have for lunch?"

Po shot Zap a look. "That's not important, Zap. Focus." He turned to the miner. "Can you take us to where you last saw the pickaxe? We'll start there."

The miner nodded eagerly, pointing toward a short rise near the riverbank. Beyond the trees, a soft white glow shimmered in the distance. "It's just over there by the crystal rocks. That's where I was working when it disappeared."

Po blinked in recognition. The glow from the crystal rocks was the same mysterious light they had seen earlier along the river.

Zap eyed the miner with curiosity. "You're sure it didn't just wander off on its own? Things tend to do that in this place."

The miner chuckled nervously but didn't seem reassured. "I sure hope not."

Po and Zap walked towards the mining area, leaving the dog to continue searching the dock. Upon approaching the mining area, the soft white glow intensified, illuminating the path ahead like a beacon. The trees gradually thinned out, revealing a clearing bathed in the ethereal light of towering crystal obelisks. The obelisks were massive, easily stretching higher than the tallest trees around.

The obelisks were arranged in a near-perfect circle, each crystal perfectly angled and positioned as if by design, though they were undoubtedly natural formations. Their surfaces sparkled with intricate, naturally occurring etchings, catching the sunlight that filtered through the trees and refracting it into dazzling rays.

In the heart of the circle, a handful of miners were scattered around the crystal obelisks. Some leaned against the base of the towering structures, while others were sprawled out on the ground, their heads resting on their mining sacks. All of them appeared to be asleep—each miner still had a firm grip on their pickaxe.

The air felt thicker here, as if charged with an invisible energy. Po strained to listen, catching faint whispers, barely audible, as if the crystals themselves were murmuring secrets. Every so often, a soft chime resonated from within one of the obelisks, and a flicker of light danced across its surface, fading as quickly as it came.

The scene was unnerving; the miners were completely still, their breathing slow and rhythmic, completely unaware of the world around them.

Zap, eyes wide with curiosity, leaned closer to Po, whispering, "I guess they are all on break."

Po frowned, scanning the scene with a deepening sense of unease. "It doesn't look like they chose to sleep. Something... feels off."

Po knelt beside one of the sleeping miners, gently shaking his shoulder. The miner stirred but didn't wake, his grip on the pickaxe tightening in response. Po stood back up, brushing his hands together, puzzled. "It's like they've been enchanted or something. Whatever's happening here, it's not natural."

Po felt a prickle of helplessness. No sword or shield could fight this kind of magic, and as much as he hated it, he knew his strength alone wasn't enough to break them free. "I should be able to help them," he muttered, frustration creeping into his voice. "But I don't even know where to start."

Zap looked around nervously, his ears twitching as if expecting something to jump out at them. "Let's just find the pickaxe and get out of here. This place is giving me the creeps."

Po and Zap moved cautiously around the circle of towering obelisks, their eyes scanning the ground for any sign of the lost pickaxe. As they neared the tallest of the obelisks, something caught Po's attention. A short distance away, at the base of the enormous crystal, was an excavated area—a roughly dug-out pit that looked like it had been worked on recently. It wasn't very deep, but it stood out from the otherwise pristine mining area.

Zap, now curious, hurried to the edge of the pit and peered down. "Look at this," he whispered. "Seems like someone's been busy digging here. What do you think they were looking for?"

Po joined him at the edge, his eyes narrowing as he took in the sight. The ground within the pit was uneven, as if whoever had been digging was in a rush. And there, at the very centre, partially buried beneath loose soil and shards of crystal, was the familiar shape of a mirror frame.

The intricate designs along the frame's edge were unmistakable—vines, creatures, and symbols similar to the ones they had encountered before. But something was wrong. The glass was shattered, its jagged pieces scattered across the ground like a broken windowpane.

Po felt his stomach twist, a wave of dread washing over him. "Another mirror..." he murmured, kneeling down for a closer look. His fingers grazed the broken shards of glass, cold and sharp against his skin, and a chill ran through him as he realized just how similar it was to the two other mirrors they'd come across. But this time, seeing it shattered filled him with a deep, unsettling fear.

Zap crouched beside him, frowning as he picked up one of the larger shards of glass, turning it over in his paw. "Why would someone smash it?" he asked, his voice low and uneasy.

Po whispered, a sense of unease settling heavily in his chest. "If someone wanted this mirror destroyed... it means they didn't just stumble upon it. They knew exactly what it was and wanted it gone." His mind raced with the implications, a dark realization dawning. "Someone's trying to cut off connections—keep people out... or trap someone inside." The thought struck him like ice, making his hands tremble slightly as he picked up a shard.

Po's gaze swept the area around the pit. The dirt was freshly disturbed, and there were clear footprints—some large and heavy, others smaller, as if multiple people had been involved. "Maybe they were trying to hide something... or prevent someone from coming through."

Po stared at the broken frame, his mind racing. Whoever had destroyed this mirror had done it with purpose and put the miners under some kind of spell. It was clear something sinister was at play. He couldn't shake the feeling that this was somehow connected to the Shadow Twins.

A heavy feeling of helplessness crept over him. They were up against forces that understood this world far better than he did, forces that could shut them out, seal them in, or manipulate their path at will. Po clenched his fists, fighting against the sense of doom that was building in his chest. "If they're willing to destroy the mirrors," he muttered, "they might destroy our only way of going home."

Zap glanced back at the miners, still fast asleep, their hands locked around their pickaxes. "So, what do we do now? Keep looking for the pickaxe?"

Po took one last look at the sleeping miners, unease gnawing at him. "We can't just leave them like this," Po muttered, his brow furrowed. He crouched down beside another miner, gently shaking his shoulder. The man stirred slightly, but didn't wake, his grip tightening around the pickaxe as though clutching onto something in a dream.

Zap frowned, his ears twitching. "I don't like it either, but whatever's keeping them asleep isn't something we've seen before. This magic feels... different." His voice dropped, as if the very air in the clearing felt heavier, more oppressive.

"Different... but stronger," Po whispered, his unease deepening. "We can't break it. Not now."

Zap's gaze lingered on the miners, frustration flickering in his eyes. "So, what? We just leave them here?"

Po hesitated, but finally nodded. "We don't have a choice. This magic—it's beyond us. We can't help them, not yet."

Zap kicked the dirt, his tail flicking with irritation. "It's not right, but I guess it makes sense."

They stood in silence for a moment. The circle of crystal obelisks loomed over them like silent sentinels.

"I'm starting to feel a little tired myself. Let's get out of here." Zap muttered, already turning back toward the path.

As they made their way back through the thinning trees, the eerie glow from the obelisks faded, swallowed by the shadows.

When they finally reached the dock, Po's heart sank. The boat was gone. The tethered rope that had held it was now frayed, swaying gently in the breeze, and the miner dog was nowhere to be seen.

Zap frowned, staring at the empty space where the boat had been. "Of course the boat has gone."

Po's eyes swept the riverbank, but there was no sign of the miner. "He must have found his pickaxe and left."

Zap's tail twitched in irritation. "Or he just stole our boat. Fantastic."

Po sighed, glancing down the riverbank where the path hugged the shoreline.

"There's a trail," Po pointed. "We'll follow it along the river. It'll take longer, but it'll get us closer to the castle."

Zap gave the trail a sceptical glance but shrugged. "Better than swimming, I guess."

Without the boat, their journey had become more arduous, but they pressed on. The path wound along the riverbank, framed by thick foliage that rustled gently in the evening breeze. Above them, the sky had started to deepen into twilight, the first stars blinking into existence.

As they walked, the faint sound of the river lapping against the shore was their only companion. Po's gaze flickered ahead, and there, in the distance, the shimmering towers of Princess Candy's castle gleamed against the darkening sky. The castle's iridescent walls sparkled like precious stones, the opalescent hues shifting from pink to violet with every angle. It was a beacon of beauty and magic, standing in stark contrast to the weight of their journey.

Zap squinted at the distant towers. "Still looks like a fancy birthday cake."

Po smiled despite himself. "Well, we're almost there."

They continued down the winding path, admiring the serene landscape surrounding them. On the riverbank, vibrant flowers began to glow faintly in the twilight, their petals opening wide to catch the last rays of sunlight. Swaying gentle, their soft hum filled the air with a melody that seemed to flow with the river.

Po's eyes softened as the calming music wrapped around them. For a moment, he allowed himself to breathe, to enjoy the small beauty that this world still offered.

Zap, though quieter than usual, still glanced back at Po with a smirk. "Hey, maybe if we ask nicely, the flowers will play us a victory song when we save the princess."

Po chuckled.

They pushed forward, the castle inching closer with every step.

XI. The Army of Light

The winding path ahead felt endless, the faint outline of Princess Candy's castle shimmering in the distance like a mirage of opalescent dreams. As Po and Zap trudged along, silence stretched between them.

Suddenly, a familiar voice broke the quiet. "Well, well, if it isn't my favourite customers!"

Po and Zap both looked up, startled. There, standing by the side of the path, was the travelling merchant, his usual wide-brimmed hat slightly askew, his brightly coloured robe swaying with each step. However, something was different this time. The merchant's face, usually filled with a playful smile, was now marked by a more serious, almost sombre expression. His sack of wares, usually brimming with an array of odd items, seemed unusually bare, save for one final crayon resting in the centre.

Zap's eyes brightened immediately. "Hey, it's you again! Still got that crayon collection?" He pointed at the single crayon, tail wagging as he added, "You're down to your last one, huh?"

The merchant nodded, his expression grim. "I must come clean. This isn't just any crayon," he said, his voice low and deliberate. "All of the crayons in the pack hold significant magical power."

Po frowned, stepping closer. "What do you mean? How can a crayon hold magic?"

The merchant's eyes narrowed slightly as he picked up the crayon, holding it out for them to see. "Each crayon in this collection is unique. This particular crayon is likened to a key."

Zap, now intrigued, leaned forward. "What does it open?"

The merchant smirked and replied in his usual, cryptic manner. "That I cannot tell you but when you see something that attracts the eye, why not draw a picture?"

Before Po or Zap could say anything further, the merchant tipped his hat and started to walk away. "Good luck," he called over his shoulder, his voice softer than usual.

As the merchant disappeared into the shadows of the trees, Po turned the blue crayon over in his hand, feeling its weight. It looked like any ordinary crayon, smooth and cylindrical, its blue paper wrapper slightly worn. It seemed ordinary, but the merchant's words seemed to echo in his mind.

As dusk settled deeper, casting a violet hue across the horizon, Po and Zap decided to set up camp in a small clearing. The air was cooler now, and the sky stretched endlessly above them, peppered with a growing blanket of stars. Po leaned against a large boulder, staring into the quiet distance, while Zap sprawled out beside the flickering campfire, his golden fur reflecting the soft glow.

For a while, they sat in silence. Above them, the sky was slowly filling with stars—an ocean of tiny lights twinkling against the deep, velvety night.

Zap broke the silence first, his voice uncharacteristically low and thoughtful. "You ever wonder what's up there?" He nodded toward the stars, his ears twitching. "I mean, really *up* there. Beyond all of this... this mess we're tangled up in."

Po blinked, caught off guard by the depth of the question. "I guess I haven't thought much about it," he admitted, leaning back to gaze at the stars with Zap. "But when you do look at it all, doesn't it feel like... everything down here, everything we've been through, is just... small in comparison?"

Zap didn't answer right away, his eyes focused intently on the sky. "Yeah," he finally said, "but sometimes I feel like we're part of something bigger. Like we're not just two guys running around trying to fix things. Maybe all the stuff we've been through—the Shadow Twins, Tezcat, the mirrors—it's all connected somehow. Maybe it's not just about us."

Po was quiet for a moment, letting Zap's words sink in. "You think... we're meant to be here? To be part of this fight?"

Zap rolled onto his back, resting his paws behind his head as he looked up at the stars. "Yeah, I do. It's like the universe is pointing us toward something, pulling us along even when we don't know where we're going." He paused, his usual playful tone softening. "I mean, think about it. What if you didn't ask that question in class? Damian and Zale wouldn't have chased you and we could've stayed out of this whole mess."

Po stared at the sky, the weight of Zap's words sinking in. "I've thought about that a lot," he admitted softly. If we hadn't have gone through that mirror, things could've been... normal."

"Normal's overrated," Zap replied, though there was no hint of his usual sarcasm. "But still, it makes you wonder, doesn't it? Like—was it chance or something else? Maybe there's a reason it was us that found the mirror."

Po shrugged, still gazing at the stars. "I don't know. But every time things get tough, we somehow seem to get through it...together."

They both stared up at the stars again, a comfortable silence settling between them. The night sky was vast, the stars twinkling like distant beacons of light, and for a moment, the weight of their journey seemed to fade.

"I used to think stars were just... dots up there," Zap said suddenly. "But now? I think they're more like... possibilities. Maybe each one is a place, or a path we could take. You know?"

Po glanced at him, raising an eyebrow. "That's... surprisingly poetic for you."

Zap snorted. "I have my moments."

Po smiled. "Possibilities, huh? I like that thought."

"Yeah," Zap said, his voice a bit softer now. "And who knows? Maybe we'll be one of those stars someday. A story someone else tells around a campfire."

The thought lingered in the air, and Po couldn't help but feel a strange sense of peace. For the first time in what felt like forever, they weren't running, fighting, or worrying about the dangers ahead. Just two friends, beneath the stars, taking a moment to rest.

And for a while, they just lay there, watching the stars until sleep finally claimed them.

The morning came softly, with the first rays of sunlight filtering through the trees, casting a golden glow over the clearing. Po stirred, blinking awake as the warmth of the sun touched his face. Zap was still curled up, his tail twitching slightly in his sleep.

Stretching, Po stood up and glanced around. It was then that something caught his eye—a strange marking on a nearby rock, faintly illuminated by the morning light.

Suddenly, Po halted. "Look," he whispered, pointing to the strange symbol carved into one of the larger rocks. It was intricate, almost runic, but unfamiliar to him.

Zap squinted, tracing the carving with his paw. "It looks like something out of a really old book."

"Let's try it," Po said, kneeling down to the dirt path beneath them. Carefully, he began to copy the symbol onto the ground, his hand steady as he sketched out each stroke with the crayon.

As soon as the final line was drawn, a deep rumbling noise echoed through the air. The ground beneath the symbol began to tremble, and a bright light shone from the cracks in the earth. Po and Zap stepped back, eyes wide as the dirt slowly crumbled away, revealing a hidden staircase descending into the ground.

Zap blinked, completely astonished. "Okay... that was cool. Didn't think a crayon could do that!"

They both cautiously approached the stairs, which led down into a narrow tunnel. Faint lights flickered along the walls as they descended.

At the bottom, they emerged into a large cavern, the rough stone transitioning into a space that felt like a tactical war room. Maps were pinned to the walls, some marked with red and blue pushpins indicating strategic points. Makeshift weapons, ranging from spears to repurposed farming tools, were lined up against stone shelves. The air was thick with the aura of strategic preparation, the quiet hum of voices discussing plans and the rustle of paper maps reinforcing the sense of an impending showdown.

Standing in the centre of the cave, bathed in the dim glow of a nearby torch, was a group of figures. The largest of them turned toward them, his green, leathery skin glinting under the light.

Captain Ezra, tall and imposing, stepped forward, his posture upright and military. He was dressed in worn but well-maintained armour, his helmet resting on a nearby table littered with maps and documents. His eyes narrowed as he sized up Po and Zap.

Behind him stood Linfer, a cat-like figure with sleek fur and sharp eyes. She had a bow slung across her back and a pair of daggers at her waist. Her gaze was cool, cautious, as if she was always looking for the quickest way to end a threat.

And standing beside her was Gunred, younger than the others, his pale skin and elven features marking him as the newest recruit. He looked eager but nervous, his hand resting on the hilt of his sword.

Ezra spoke first, his voice low and commanding. "Who are you, and how did you find us?"

Po took a step forward, holding up his hands in a gesture of peace. "We're not your enemies. We're here to stop the Shadow Twins."

Ezra's eyes flicked between Po and Zap, his expression hard. "You know of Tezcat, then?"

Po nodded. "We've encountered him before. Barely made it out alive. He's more powerful than we imagined—and he's getting stronger."

Ezra, still harbouring suspicions about the two newcomers, scrutinized Po. "Getting stronger? In what way?"

Po paused for a moment to gather his thoughts. "We've learned a lot about how Tezcat and his brother are moving through the kingdom. They're using mirrors—magical ones. They can travel instantly between locations, sending their armies to destroy anything that shines."

Linfer's ears twitched at the mention of the mirrors. "Mirrors? That's how they've been staying one step ahead of us..."

Ezra frowned, processing the information. "We've been fighting Tezcat's forces for months, but every time we strike, they seem to know exactly where to counter us."

Gunred, clearly eager to contribute, piped up. "We've heard rumours about Tezcat destroying the sources of light in the kingdom—places like Podkin & Ham's Light Factory. They're trying to wipe out anything that could resist them."

Po exchanged a glance with Zap. "That's what we were thinking, too."

Linfer, ever the pragmatist, crossed her arms. "So, what's your plan? You can't expect to defeat the Shadow Twins with just the two of you."

Po took a deep breath, glancing at the members of the resistance. "You're right. We need your help. If we can destroy the mirrors, we can slow them down. We can make it harder for them to move their armies. But we can't do it alone."

Ezra stared at Po for a long moment before finally nodding. "If what you're saying is true, then you've given us the first real chance we've had to strike back."

Ezra then laid out a plan. He turned to Gunred with determination. "First, we need to gather the other members of the resistance. Once we've done this, we will create a distraction by storming the courtyard."

Zap, being uncharacteristically quiet, trembled slightly. "What are we supposed to do? I don't have a weapon, and even if I did, I don't have thumbs to use it."

Linfer uncrossed her arms and glanced at Po and Zap. "There's a secret passage beneath the castle. An old escape route from the days when Princess Candy's ancestors ruled. Most have forgotten it exists—except for a few of us who've studied the kingdom's history closely."

Ezra gave a firm nod. "That passage is how you'll get inside without alerting the shadow guards. Once you're in, your mission is clear—find every mirror you can and destroy it."

Gunred, standing off to the side, shifted nervously. "But... won't that leave us trapped? If you destroy the mirrors, how do we escape?"

Linfer scoffed, crossing her arms again. "Destroying the mirrors is reckless. What if they have more traps in place? We'll be walking right into their hands, just like last time."

"We have no other choice. If we don't move now, we lose any element of surprise." Ezra said firmly.

Linfer clenched her fist, slamming it down with force onto the table in front of her. "Surprise? The last 'surprise' cost us four good soldiers, Ezra! We can't afford to keep fighting blindly."

Gunred stood forward, his voice still shaky. "My family... they're still out there. They were taken when the shadow creatures attacked. I thought I could protect them by joining the resistance, but sometimes it feels like there's no hope."

Linfer, lowered her guard and spoke less harshly. "We've all got stakes in this."

The room went silent for a moment as the reality of the situation sank in.

Ezra then turned toward Gunred and gave him a nod. "Prepare the others. We'll move out shortly."

Linfer gave a quick nod to Po and Zap, then turned toward the rear of the cavern. "Follow me. The entrance to the passage is not far."

Without hesitation, she led them down a narrow corridor that twisted and turned.

After a few minutes, they reached a small, concealed door carved into the stone. Linfer pulled back a thick vine that was draped over the entrance, revealing the hidden passage.

"This will take us beneath the castle," Linfer whispered, her eyes glinting with resolve. "Once we're inside, there's no turning back."

Po and Zap exchanged a glance, their determination mirrored in each other's eyes. "We're ready," Po said quietly.

Linfer pushed the door open, and together they stepped into the darkness, the path ahead leading straight to Princess Candy's castle.

XII. Hall of Mirrors

A damp chill settled over Po, sinking into his bones as he, Zap, and Linfer wound through the narrow stone passageway beneath the castle. Shadows crept along the walls, flickering like uncertain spirits caught between worlds. Each footfall seemed too loud, echoing down the stone-walled corridor, which twisted and turned through the ancient castle foundations. The only light came from the torch Linfer carried, casting an eerie glow over their faces.

Zap kept his voice to a tense whisper, his golden eyes glinting nervously in the half-light. "So... just to be clear—this passage leads somewhere useful, right?"

Linfer gave a slight nod, her eyes fixed forward. "It leads into the castle's southern wing, near the main chambers. Tezcat... he doesn't know it's here." Her voice was steady, but Po could sense the strain underneath.

They walked in silence for a few moments before Zap, his curiosity getting the best of him, sidled a bit closer to Linfer. "You've, uh, you've done this sort of thing before, haven't you?"

Linfer glanced at him, her usual stoic expression softening slightly. "You could say that," she replied, her voice barely louder than a whisper.

Zap perked up, sensing an opening. "So... what's your story then? I mean, we know you're good with those daggers, and you've got that 'been-there, done-that' look." He paused, then added, "So, why did you join the resistance?"

Linfer hesitated, her fingers tightening around the hilt of one of her daggers. Po glanced over, sensing her reluctance, but she sighed and nodded, a faint shadow crossing her face.

"There was a time, long before all this," she began, her voice almost too quiet to hear, "when I never thought I'd be fighting in a resistance army or risking my life in some damp castle corridor." She managed a weak smile, though her eyes remained distant. "I was a simple hunter, back in my village. I loved the quiet—just me, the trees, and the sound of leaves underfoot. I knew every trail in that forest, every bird call."

Zap's eyes widened. "A hunter? So, you've always been able to... you know." He mimed throwing a dagger, grinning despite the tension.

Linfer chuckled softly, and for a moment, the war-worn look in her eyes softened. "It was mostly my bow back then. I was fast, good with tracking." Her smile faded as her gaze dropped to the floor. "One day, my brother—his name was Merric—was with me. We were just scouting, keeping an eye out for a wolf pack that had moved in close to the village. Harmless enough, usually. But that day... I don't know what was different. Maybe they were hungrier, desperate." She paused, the memory sharp and painful. "We were surrounded before I could even get an arrow off. Merric was only fifteen..."

Zap's ears flattened as he whispered, "I'm... I'm sorry, Linfer."

Linfer nodded slightly, her expression hardening. "That day changed me. It made me realize how quickly everything can be taken from you. And when I heard that Tezcat and Epial had begun spreading their shadows, destroying villages without mercy—I couldn't stay out of it. I had to fight for those who couldn't. People like my brother."

The corridor seemed to close in, the weight of her words hanging heavy in the air. Even Po, who'd only known Linfer since that morning, felt as if he were seeing a different side of her—a side forged by loss and unyielding purpose.

"You fight for him, then," Po murmured, breaking the silence. "Every day."

She nodded, a look of fierce determination in her eyes. "And for anyone else who lost someone they loved to Tezcat's darkness." She straightened, her grip on the torch resolute.

Zap glanced at her, a mixture of admiration and sadness in his gaze. "You're a lot tougher than I gave you credit for."

Linfer offered a small, sad smile. "We all have reasons to fight, Zap. I just carry mine with me every day."

Suddenly, a distant, thunderous crash reverberated through the stone walls, causing a fine mist of dust to rain down on them. Po's heart skipped; he recognized it as the sound of a battering ram slamming into the castle's outer gates. Muffled shouts soon followed, the rallying cries of the Army of Light echoing aboveground as Ezra and the others launched their assault on the courtyard.

"We're out of time," Linfer whispered, quickening her pace.

As they hurried through the narrow passage, another heavy thud shook the corridor, and for a brief moment, the sound of clanging swords and the fierce battle cries of soldiers filtered through the stone above them. Po could imagine the scene: the resistance fighters charging forward, weapons raised, their hearts steeled against the overwhelming darkness. The courtyard, once a silent fortress, was now alive with the shouts of battle, the clash of steel against steel, and the roar of defiance.

A distant, booming voice rang out, likely Ezra, rallying his soldiers in the midst of chaos. "Hold your ground! For the kingdom!"

Po could almost see Captain Ezra's determined face, standing at the forefront with his weapon drawn, urging his soldiers forward as they pushed against Tezcat's forces. There was no turning back for them either. Their mission was to create enough havoc to keep Tezcat's guards from descending into the castle and discovering Po, Linfer, and Zap.

The sound of a massive crash echoed through the corridor, louder this time. Po pictured one of the castle's fortified walls giving way, the brave soldiers pouring in to confront Tezcat's forces. They would be outnumbered, and many wouldn't make it back out—but the Army of Light pressed on, their loyalty to the kingdom unbreakable.

The sound of the battle grew muffled again as Po, Linfer, and Zap wound further into the castle. Each step brought them nearer to Tezcat's territory, where each corner might reveal a shadow guard, or worse—the Shadow Twin himself.

When they reached the end of the passageway, Linfer raised a finger to her lips, signalling silence, and pushed against a heavy stone slab at the end of the tunnel. It slid back with a low, scraping groan, and she carefully peered through the opening before beckoning them to follow. Po climbed through into a room cluttered with stacks of dusty crates and covered furniture, tucked away in the castle's forgotten wing. Linfer quickly shut the hidden entrance behind them.

A faint, ghostly light filtered in from a narrow, high window. Shadows danced along the walls as the wind outside moaned.

Zap's gaze darted around as he took in the room. His voice was barely above a murmur, but Po could hear the edge of nervousness in it. "So, what exactly are we expecting here? Besides... you know, guards who want to crush us?"

Linfer's expression was grim. "Tezcat is a creature of deception. Mirrors are his portals. If there are any, we'll likely find them in the rooms closest to his quarters. But we'll need to be careful."

Zap gave a small nod, his tail stiff as he crouched low, scanning the dimly lit room. "All I'm saying is, if anything comes at us from a dark corner, I'm outta here."

Despite the tension, Po managed a small smile. "You're not going anywhere without us."

Linfer then beckoned Po and Zap over to a worn, wooden door, turning the aged handle. Po and Zap followed Linfer out of the room, into a seemingly endless corridor.

As they made their way along the corridor, every door seemed to hide a potential threat, and Po's shoulders tightened with each step. The shadows on the walls seemed to shift and crawl, as if watching their progress. After passing several closed doors, Linfer paused outside one particularly grand set of double doors. They were carved with swirling patterns that seemed to pulse and shift in the low light.

Linfer pressed her ear to the door, listening intently. After a long moment, she whispered, "I think this is it... they're beyond these doors."

Po took a deep breath, glancing at Zap, who gave a small, determined nod. With a final look at Linfer, Po pushed the doors open.

They stepped into a grand hall, its high ceiling arching above them, cloaked in shadows. Along the walls were rows of tall mirrors, each standing as if part of an elaborate display, their gilt frames shimmering faintly in the dim light. Each mirror was marked with a nameplate, the destinations they connected to etched in bold brass letters. Po's gaze swept over the nameplates attached to each frame, and he felt a chill when he recognized some of the names: *Solaris Athenaeum. Amberstone Ascent. Podkin & Ham's Light Factory.*

Every mirror represented a place they'd visited, and likely more they hadn't. He glanced at Linfer, whose face had hardened.

"These..." Linfer whispered, scanning the mirrors with disdain. "They're his anchors, his way of spreading his power over the entire kingdom."

Po felt a deep anger rise in his chest, mingling with fear. The Hall of Mirrors wasn't just a tool; it was a symbol of Tezcat's stranglehold over the kingdom, his reach stretching farther than they'd ever realized.

"So," Zap muttered, swallowing hard, "do we just start smashing?"

Linfer shook her head. "Not yet. If we start breaking them randomly, we risk alerting Tezcat."

Po held up his sword, feeling its familiar weight. "But we need to do something." His voice was steady, but doubt edged his words. "If we don't stop him now..."

Without further hesitation, Po swung his sword into the nearest mirror. It shattered with a sharp crack, the fragments hitting the ground and disintegrating into shadows. A faint hiss filled the air, echoing across the room like the last breath of a dying creature. Po's chest tightened; he could feel the weight of each mirror they destroyed, as if with each shatter, a piece of Tezcat's control over the kingdom weakened.

Linfer was already moving to the next mirror, her daggers glinting as she slashed through the glass. "Keep going!" she shouted. "If we disrupt enough, it could—"

But her words were cut short as a low, cold voice filled the chamber, sending a shiver down Po's spine.

"Well, well," Tezcat's voice drawled, smooth and dripping with disdain. "Uninvited guests causing such a mess? How inconsiderate."

They turned to see a mirror in the far corner ripple like disturbed water, and from its depths, Tezcat emerged, his figure tall and imposing, shadows curling around him like living creatures. His eyes glittered with cold amusement as he surveyed the room.

Zap bared his teeth, his hackles rising. "Yeah? Well, your mirrors are ugly anyway," he snapped, but Po could hear the tension in his voice.

Tezcat's gaze settled on Zap, a smirk curling at his lips. "Be careful not to bite little pet, or I may have to put you down." His eyes flicked toward Po, who was now lingering onto his sword and shield. "And you—destroying such antiques? I didn't place you as a criminal."

Po lifted his sword, meeting Tezcat's cold stare. "You can taunt us all you want, but we're ending this. We'll break every mirror, cut off your control, and free this kingdom from you and your brother."

Tezcat's smile twisted into something darker. "Epial travels North as we speak, spreading his influence across all six kingdoms." His eyes gleamed with a sinister satisfaction. "And while you're so fixated on stopping me, the bigger picture eludes you entirely."

Linfer shot Po a warning glance. "Don't waste words on him," she muttered. "He's stalling."

But Tezcat's expression remained calm, his gaze never leaving Po's. "Tell me, Po, do you truly think you can save anyone by breaking a few mirrors? The wheels started turning long before you arrived in the fourth kingdom." With a flick of his hand, the remaining mirrors began to shimmer, and shadowy shapes started to form within the glass—figures emerging like dark phantoms from the mirrors' depths.

One by one, shadow guards, beasts, and other monstrous creatures stepped out, the creatures appearing in silence but radiating menace. Each figure had an unnatural, almost liquid darkness about it, their eyes glowing faintly red.

Po felt a jolt of panic but forced himself to stay calm. He raised the shield, bracing himself. "Linfer, Zap—stay close."

Tezcat's eyes glinted with satisfaction as he watched the creatures surround them. "I hope you realize how futile this is. You're not heroes. You're merely... inconveniences." He waved a hand lazily, and the creatures lunged forward as one.

The first beast leapt at Po, its massive claws swinging down toward him. He raised the dragon-tooth shield just in time, absorbing the blow as a surge of energy flowed into the shield, making it glow brighter. With a swift motion, he swung back, sending the creature stumbling into one of the mirrors, where it vanished in a puff of dark smoke.

Zap darted around, snapping at the heels of another guard to keep him distracted. Meanwhile, Linfer moved with deadly precision, her daggers flashing as she struck down a shadowy creature, her movements as fluid as water.

But with every creature they fought, two more seemed to take its place, emerging from the endless row of mirrors like a never-ending nightmare. The sheer number of enemies was overwhelming, and it wasn't long before Po felt fatigue seeping into his bones, the weight of each block and swing growing heavier.

Linfer, panting heavily, cast a desperate look at Po. "We're outmatched. We can't take them all down like this."

Po gritted his teeth, casting a glance around the room. Zap's fur was slick with sweat, his eyes darting nervously as he tried to fend off a guard twice his size. Linfer's movements were slowing, her usually swift strikes becoming laboured.

Tezcat watched the scene unfold with satisfaction, his gaze cold and calculating. "Do you see now? You're nothing more than ants, trying to fight a god."

Po felt a wave of despair, but he pushed it down, his resolve hardening. "Linfer," he said, his voice low but urgent. "There has to be a way out."

Linfer's gaze swept the room, landing on one of the mirrors near the far wall. Her eyes narrowed with sudden resolve. "There's one way, but... it's risky."

Zap, darting away from another guard's swing, called out, "Risky is better than dead, right?"

Linfer nodded, her jaw set. "This mirror here," she panted, cutting down another shadow beast as it lunged at her, "it should lead somewhere far from Tezcat's reach. But you two need to go now."

Po's eyes widened in alarm as he stepped closer. "Wait—you're coming too. We're not leaving you here."

Linfer gave a small, sad smile, a depth of sorrow and resolve flickering in her eyes. "One of us has to stay, or Tezcat will follow. There are too many of them, Po. If we don't stop him now, he'll only get stronger. You have to keep going. Destroy more mirrors. Fight for the kingdom."

"No!" Po's voice broke, his hand reaching out to her. He could feel his chest tightening, the thought of leaving her behind tearing at him. "There has to be another way!"

Linfer placed a hand on his shoulder, her grip firm. "I made a vow to protect this kingdom... just like you did. And sometimes, that means sacrifices. Go. Don't look back."

Zap's ears drooped, his eyes glistening as he realized what Linfer was doing. "Linfer..."

She looked down at him, her expression softening for just a moment. "Take care of each other. And if you get the chance, make sure Tezcat pays for this."

Po hesitated, every fibre in his being wanting to stay, to fight with her. But Linfer's gaze hardened. "Now, Po. For the kingdom."

Reluctantly, with every step feeling heavier than the last, Po grasped Zap's fur, pulling him toward the mirror. With one last, pained look at Linfer, he stepped through the glass, feeling a chill sweep over him as they passed through the portal.

The last thing Po saw was Linfer standing tall, her daggers flashing as she faced Tezcat and the endless tide of shadow creatures, her figure small but defiant. Then, in a final, decisive motion, she slashed at the mirror's frame, and the portal shattered into a million shards, her image fading away as the glass broke.

In the silence that followed, Po found himself and Zap alone in an unknown place, far from anywhere they had been before, the memory of Linfer's last stand etched deeply into his heart. He clenched his fists, a vow burning in his chest.

"We'll make this count," he whispered, as Zap huddled close beside him, their shared grief and determination binding them in silence.

13

XIII. Sanctuary

Mist clung to the ground like a second skin, wrapping Po and Zap in a damp, ghostly veil as they wandered through the dense forest bordering the Fourth Kingdom. The towering, ancient trees stood silent, their trunks twisted and gnarled, as if watching the two outsiders trespass into their domain. The faint glow of bioluminescent moss scattered light through the underbrush, casting an otherworldly glow on their faces. They hadn't spoken in some time; the silence, heavy and unbreakable, mirrored the lingering ache in their hearts.

Po's hand hovered over the hilt of his sword, fingers wrapped tightly around it as if holding on to something that was slipping from his grasp. He could still see the last image of Linfer's face as she made her stand against Tezcat. Her final words echoed in his mind, urging him to move forward, to make her sacrifice count. But the weight of it all dragged him down; a nagging feeling that he should have done more.

After a while, Zap broke the silence, his voice uncharacteristically subdued. "Po... do you think we could have saved her? That maybe if we had been faster or... I don't know, maybe smarter, she'd still be here?"

Po kept his gaze fixed on the misty ground, the cold biting deeper as he thought of how to answer. "I keep replaying it, Zap. Wondering what we could've done differently. She was brave... so much braver than I was. She knew what she was getting into, but..." He took a shaky breath. "It doesn't make it easier. And somehow, it just doesn't feel fair." He could still feel the weight of Linfer's final look—unwavering trust, and something like forgiveness. But he wasn't sure he deserved it.

Zap nodded, his eyes fixed on the shadows as they walked. "She believed in you, though, Po. You saw it in the way she looked at you, like she knew you'd figure it all out." His ears drooped, and he slowed his pace to match Po's. "But it's just—losing people, Po, it hurts more than I ever thought it could. I don't know if I was ready for any of this."

Po stopped, placing a hand on Zap's back. He forced a small smile, though it didn't quite reach his eyes. "None of us were, Zap. But that's why we keep going. For Linfer. And for everyone else who's still fighting." He tightened his grip on his sword's hilt, as if drawing strength from it. "We owe it to them to keep pushing forward, no matter how much it hurts."

Zap gave a quiet, determined nod, but the sorrow lingered between them, unspoken yet profoundly shared. They started walking again, their silence now a gentle truce with the grief they carried.

The forest grew denser, and soon they found themselves in a maze of towering roots and thorny brambles. Each direction looked the same—a seemingly endless fog-coated wilderness. The bioluminescent moss pulsed faintly, casting shifting shadows that danced like spectres on the twisted trees.

Zap sighed, peering through the mist. "Any idea where we are? Or where we're going?"

Po shook his head. "Not a clue. I think we're still somewhere on the northern edge of the Kingdom. But honestly, I wouldn't be surprised if we've wandered right back to where we started."

Zap chuckled dryly, his usual spark dulled by the weight of their journey. "You know, for once, I wouldn't mind a sign.

Something that just says, *This way to victory*." He kicked a small stone off the path, watching as it disappeared into the fog. "But I guess that would be asking too much, wouldn't it?"

As they continued to make their way through the mist, Zap suddenly froze, his ears pricking up. Po followed his gaze and saw a small creature, no bigger than a rabbit, darting between the trees. It had purple and pink fur that shimmered faintly, long tufted ears, and a feathery tail that glowed softly in the dim light. Its eyes, wide and bright, fixed on Po and Zap, frozen in place as though uncertain whether to flee or stay.

Po slowly crouched down, reaching a hand out, his voice gentle. "Hey there, little dude... it's okay. We're not here to hurt you."

The creature tilted its head, watching Po with a wary curiosity. For a brief moment, it seemed to consider trusting him, its body relaxing just slightly. But then, as if spooked by an invisible threat, it scurried off into the underbrush, disappearing from view.

Zap blinked, glancing at Po. "Well, that was... something. Should we follow it?"

Po shrugged, a flicker of curiosity in his eyes. "I mean, it's the only lead we've got. And it's got to know this place better than we do."

With a shared nod, they set off after the creature, carefully weaving through the twisted undergrowth. The forest seemed to part slightly in their wake, as if guiding them forward. They followed the faint glow of the creature's tail, winding through narrow trails and ducking under low-hanging branches.

The surroundings gradually shifted, the mist thinning and the trees growing taller, their branches arching overhead to form a natural cathedral. They emerged into a secluded glade, where the air felt warmer, the sunlight breaking through the canopy in dappled patches. A faint scent of wildflowers filled the air, and the soft sound of trickling water added a peaceful rhythm to the silence. At the centre of the glade was a crystal-clear pool, its surface so still that it reflected the sky above, unmarred by the darkness that lingered beyond.

Po felt a sense of calm wash over him as he took in the sight. There was a stillness to the place, an aura of safety that felt almost like a gentle embrace. It was a sanctuary, hidden and untouched by the shadows that had consumed the rest of the kingdom.

But it wasn't just the glade that caught their attention. By the edge of the pool stood a woman, her figure half-hidden by the trees. She held a staff in one hand, her posture tense as she watched them approach, her gaze sharp and wary.

Zap's eyes darted to Po, whispering, "Who do you think she is? And why does she look like she's about to run us through with that staff?"

Po stepped forward cautiously, raising his hands to show he meant no harm. "I'm sorry if we startled you. We didn't mean to intrude... we're just a bit lost."

The woman's gaze didn't soften, her grip on the staff unwavering. "Lost, are you? People don't usually wander into places like this unless they're looking for something."

Zap, sensing the tension, gave a small, nervous laugh. "Well, technically, we're looking for... directions? Or, you know, any hint as to where we are." His voice grew quieter. "I'm guessing this isn't the Kingdom's welcome centre."

The woman's stern expression flickered, a hint of amusement breaking through her guarded demeanour. "This isn't a place you'll find on any map. It's a sanctuary, hidden for those who need refuge." Her eyes narrowed slightly. "So, tell me, what brings you here?"

Po took a deep breath, choosing his words carefully. "We're on a journey to stop Tezcat and Epial. We fought Tezcat at the castle but... things didn't go as planned. We lost a friend, and now we're just trying to find a way forward."

The woman's gaze softened, a shadow of sorrow passing over her face. She lowered her staff slightly, though her posture remained cautious. "The Army of Light has spoken of two travellers who defied the Shadow Twins at every turn. A boy and a dog. Stories of your battles have spread further than you think."

Po blinked in surprise, glancing at Zap. "Stories? About us?"

The woman's gaze met his, and for the first time, Po caught a glimpse of something familiar in her eyes—strength, determination, and a deep-seated sorrow. "Yes. I've heard your tales... Po and Zap, isn't it?"

Po nodded, still processing the revelation. "That's us. But... who are you?"

The woman hesitated, as if weighing her words carefully. Finally, she sighed, lowering her staff completely. "I am Princess Candy."

Zap's mouth dropped open, and he glanced back and forth between Po and the princess, speechless. "You're... the princess? But... you're supposed to be at the castle."

A bitter smile tugged at the corner of her mouth. "I was. But Tezcat's shadows came too quickly. The castle fell before I could rally the guards, and the kingdom fell with it." She looked away, her voice softening. " I thought I could protect my people, that I could make a difference. But all I could do was run. I barely escaped. And I've been here ever since, waiting, hoping the Army of Light would come."

Po's expression shifted, his heart aching at the sorrow in her voice. "We didn't know... we thought you were still trapped."

The princess's gaze hardened, her eyes filled with a fierce resolve. "I may be hidden, but I am not defeated. I'm only here because it's where I can do the most good—for now. I'm not willing to throw away my life for nothing."

Zap nodded, his respect for the princess growing. "You've been through a lot. And, honestly... we could use someone like you by our side."

The princess hesitated, her gaze sweeping over them both. "It isn't safe for anyone here. The shadows stretch far beyond the castle, and the Fourth Kingdom isn't the only one under threat." She paused, her eyes shadowed with a distant pain. "The Shadow Twins are not ordinary enemies. They were both men of talent and ambition, before they turned to darkness."

Po's eyes widened, his interest piqued. "What do you mean?"

The princess sighed, sinking onto a fallen log by the pool. "Epial was once an apprentice to the renowned sorcerer, Xeor. He trained under him at the Solaris Athenaeum and was known as a prodigy. But his thirst for power grew, and he began seeking rare, ancient magic—forms of shadow and forgotten magic that were forbidden by Xeor." She closed her eyes, a sorrowful expression crossing her face. "Epial's hunger for knowledge became his obsession. Eventually, he embraced shadow magic and convinced his brother, Tezcat, to join him."

Zap's ears perked up, his curiosity piqued. "So, what about Tezcat? Was he always... like this?"

A flicker of pain crossed the princess's face. "No. Tezcat was a different story. He was a brilliant engineer, and one of the original founders of what is now known as Podkin & Ham's Light Factory. In the beginning, he worked alongside them, hoping to use light energy to change the kingdom for the better. But he saw light as a weapon, a tool to exert control. When he suggested harnessing the energy to create powerful weapons, Podkin and Ham refused. They dismissed his ideas and eventually, they forced him out."

Zap's eyes widened. "So he... went rogue?"

The princess nodded. "Angry, humiliated, and now resentful of the people he had once hoped to help, Tezcat turned to Epial. Together, they vowed to build a kingdom where they would wield power and control, free from the moral restraints that had held them back. And now..." She paused, her voice trembling slightly. "Now they are willing to destroy everything and everyone in their path to see that vision fulfilled."

Po felt a chill run down his spine as the pieces came together. "They're not just after the kingdom—they're after control. Complete control."

The princess met his gaze, her eyes fierce and unyielding. "Which is why we have to stop them. I may be hidden, but I will not remain idle. I've been planning, waiting for the moment to strike."

A glint of determination sparked in Po's eyes. "Then we're not alone. We can still fight."

The princess allowed herself a small, hopeful smile. "No, Po. We're not alone. And with allies like you two... there's still hope for the kingdom."

The princess's expression softened, and she let out a small sigh as her gaze drifted to the glade around them. "I wasn't always alone here, you know. A few days ago, Podkin and Ham came through. They were here and gone before I could even grasp what they were saying, but there was no mistaking them."

Po and Zap exchanged a surprised glance, leaning in as the princess continued.

"*The* Podkin and Ham?" Po asked, feeling his curiosity ignite. They'd heard so much about the quirky inventors before, but the idea of them hiding in a remote sanctuary seemed as improbable as it was fascinating.

The princess nodded, a soft smile gracing her lips. "Yes, Podkin and Ham. They showed up looking like they'd been through a storm—scuffed up, bags half-spilled, talking so fast I could barely keep up." She shook her head in amusement. "They're quite a pair, aren't they? Always full of energy, and always up to something. They barely stopped to rest, though. They were so preoccupied, talking about some tree."

Zap tilted his head, a glint of interest in his eyes. "A tree? That sounds... random, even for them. Did they say what kind of tree?"

The princess chuckled, her gaze distant as if trying to recall their whirlwind visit. "They were speaking so quickly, I could hardly follow. Something about a tree. They seemed to think it was very important." She looked at Po and Zap, her tone growing serious. "Whatever they were searching for, it was clearly no ordinary tree." Her eyes flickered with an intensity that made Po shiver, as if she knew that this tree, whatever it was, held secrets that could change the fate of the kingdom.

Po's mind raced, trying to connect the dots. "Did they say where they were going next?"

"They didn't stay long enough for me to ask. But they did mention something about the 'Protectors of the Woods'." She lowered her voice, an expression of admiration in her eyes. "I was too young to understand it fully, but Podkin and Ham... they've always had this way of making you believe anything's possible. They don't just make things; they inspire people. And when they left, they looked determined, like they were about to find something that could change everything."

Zap's ears perked up, his usual light-hearted tone replaced with sincere wonder. "Everyone around here seems to love them. National Treasures, huh?"

The princess smiled, a bit wistfully. "They've touched the lives of everyone in the kingdom, even if most people don't realize it. When I was a child, Podkin once came to the castle to fix an old fountain in the gardens. He spent hours tinkering with it, and when he finally finished, it didn't just work; it played music. Beautiful, enchanting music that danced with the water." She glanced at Po, her expression softening. "Podkin told me that even the smallest things we make are pieces of ourselves, and those pieces live on in ways we can't always see."

Po felt a pang of respect and wonder as he imagined the scene. "They're not just light makers. They're artists."

The princess nodded. "Exactly. And Ham's another story altogether—he was the quieter one, but he had a gift for turning ideas into something even more magical. I think Podkin would come up with all the wild ideas, and Ham... Ham would make them real. Together, they were unstoppable."

Zap glanced over at Po, a look of renewed determination on his face. "We can't just let them keep running. If they're still out there, we have to find them and see if they'll help us. It sounds like they're after something big, something that could be a game-changer."

Po's thoughts raced. He knew Zap was right. The very idea that Podkin and Ham might be out there, tracking down something that could turn the tide against the Shadow Twins, sparked a beacon of hope. But he couldn't shake the uncertainty, the feeling that they were still missing something crucial. Could it really be enough? Against enemies like Tezcat and Epial, a mysterious tree and a pair of eccentric inventors seemed a fragile hope, but it was all they had.

"Did they say anything else?" Po asked the princess, his voice a mixture of hope and urgency. "About what they were working on, or... how they planned to stop Tezcat and Epial?"

The princess looked thoughtful for a moment, her gaze turning inward as she sifted through her memories of their brief encounter. "Not directly, but they seemed... almost exhilarated by the danger they were in, if that makes any sense. They didn't treat it as a burden. In fact, they said it was something they'd been preparing for, for a long time. They kept saying, 'We're close,' and 'Once we find it...'"

Zap tilted his head, his brow furrowing. "So... this thing they're working on, is it a weapon?"

The princess shook her head, her gaze distant. "Podkin and Ham never wanted to make weapons, not even when the kingdom was under siege. I think whatever they're after, it's meant to be something... different."

Po's pulse quickened as the pieces began to form a hazy picture in his mind. "If they've been working on something to counter Tezcat's shadow magic, it could explain why they're in hiding. Tezcat would see them as a threat."

The princess's face grew serious. "That's what I'm afraid of. If the Shadow Twins are aware of Podkin and Ham's work, they won't stop until they've found a way to silence them. And the kingdom will suffer for it." A flicker of fear crossed her face, a vulnerability that made her seem, just for a moment, not a princess, but a young woman who'd lost everything.

Zap scratched his head, his ears twitching as he thought. "Earlier, you mentioned something about the 'Protectors of the woods'?"

The princess nodded slowly. "They are a growing influence, spreading across the kingdoms. I don't know much about them, but they seem to be very protective of something. If Podkin and Ham are looking for them, maybe you should seek them out, too." Her gaze sharpened, as if remembering something. "The Protectors have their own ways, ancient and secretive. If you find them, tread carefully. They do not trust easily."

Zap let out a long breath, shaking his head. "I just hope they're safe. If Tezcat finds them first..."

The princess's eyes darkened. "Then it may be too late for all of us."

A sombre silence fell between them as they each absorbed the weight of her words. The flicker of hope, though small, seemed to waver against the grim reality they faced.

Po placed a reassuring hand on Zap's shoulder, a quiet determination filling his gaze. "We'll find them, Zap. Somehow, we'll make sure they're safe, and we'll see this through.

Princess Candy, resolved to assist them on their quest, pointed to the map. "You will need to journey across the sea to reach the Fifth Kingdom." She gently traced her finger across the map. "The Four Winds Coast is nearby. You should find a boat there."

"Then we will head to the Four Winds Coast," Zap declared with determination.

"But for now, we rest," Po added, yawning.

As the sun began to dip below the trees, casting a soft glow over the hidden sanctuary, Po, Zap, and the princess sat together, their resolve solidified, united by their shared mission. The light of the setting sun cast long shadows across the glade, but within them, Po saw something new—a flicker of resilience, a spark of defiance that the shadows couldn't touch. For the first time in days, he felt like they might have a chance.

14

XIV. Edge of The World

Leaving the protective shadows of the forest behind, Po and Zap stepped onto unfamiliar terrain. The dense canopy overhead gave way to wide, open skies, and the gradual sound of crashing waves replaced the quiet rustle of leaves. Ahead, the horizon stretched endlessly, blurred by the thick, salt-laden mist carried on powerful gusts from the sea. As they walked, the forest grew sparse until it finally surrendered to rough terrain of windswept rocks and coarse grasses clinging stubbornly to the earth. The air here was sharper, biting with each gust and filling their lungs with the briny tang of the ocean.

"Feels like the edge of the world," Po murmured, his voice nearly lost in the roar of the distant surf. He could feel the raw power of the coast even from here, like a silent challenge daring them to press forward. A flicker of unease settled in his chest, as if the landscape itself were warning them of the journey ahead.

"Feels different out here, doesn't it?" Zap said, flicking his ears as if listening to something only he could hear. His usual confidence was dampened, his eyes darting cautiously to the shadows beyond the rocks.

They climbed over jagged rocks, each step bringing them closer to the sea. When they crested the last rise, the coastline unfolded before them in full, an untamed expanse of water and rock. Towering waves rolled in, crashing violently against the shore and sending sprays of cold seawater high into the air, where they glittered momentarily in the faint sunlight before vanishing. Po shielded his eyes from the whipping sand and looked to the horizon, feeling a strange mix of awe and anticipation. It was beautiful, yes—but also treacherous, as if the sea itself held secrets it wasn't ready to share.

Po scanned the shoreline, catching sight of faint traces of smoke rising from behind a cluster of wind-battered rocks. He nudged Zap, who was eyeing the waves warily, his fur buffeted by the strong wind.

"See that?" Po said, pointing toward the smoke. "Looks like someone's got a camp over there."

Zap squinted, his eyes narrowed against the wind. "Who would be out here in the middle of nowhere?" he asked, doubt clear in his voice. "Unless they're hiding from something."

They pushed forward, climbing over slippery rocks as the wind howled around them, nearly knocking them off balance. As they rounded the cluster of boulders, they spotted a makeshift camp sheltered from the worst of the wind. Three figures huddled around a small, flickering fire—an elven woman, her face weary but kind; a young child, clinging to her side; and a soldier with a rough bandage wound tightly around his side, his gaze sharp and alert even in exhaustion.

The woman spotted them first, her eyes widening slightly as she instinctively pulled her child closer. The soldier's hand went to the hilt of his dagger, his posture tense. Po raised his hands, palms open in a gesture of peace.

"Please don't be afraid," Po said, pitching his voice against the wind. "We're just passing... seeking safe passage to the Fifth Kingdom."

The soldier, a broad-shouldered man with piercing green eyes, sized them up, then gave a small nod. He relaxed, though his hand remained close to his weapon.

"Usually, people are travelling away from the Fifth Kingdom," he replied, his voice deep and gravelly. "Name's Starlin. This here is Evelyn, and her boy, Anrar."

Evelyn gave them a slight, cautious smile, her eyes warm but guarded as she studied Po and Zap. She looked tired, her face etched with lines of worry, but there was a resilience there, too, as if she had long ago learned how to bear burdens that others would shy away from.

The child, Anrar, peeked out from behind his mother, his large, curious eyes darting from Po to Zap. Po offered him a reassuring smile, and Anrar took a tentative step closer, though he clutched a small leatherbound writing pad in his hand.

"I'm Po," he said gently, nodding toward his friend. "And this is Zap."

Zap waved a paw, his face bright despite the wind and the tension. "Nice to meet you all. Hope you don't mind—this wind's giving me the chills."

Evelyn exchanged a glance with Starlin, who gave a brief nod. She motioned for them to sit by the fire. "You're welcome to join us," she said softly. "The coast isn't an easy place to find rest."

Po and Zap settled close to the fire, grateful for its warmth. The fire crackled softly, its orange glow casting dancing shadows on their faces. Evelyn had a faint floral scent clinging to her, a subtle souvenir of the Fifth Kingdom's lush fields. It felt oddly comforting, providing Po with a sense of calm he hadn't known he needed.

As they warmed themselves, Po glanced at Starlin, noticing the dried blood on his tunic. "Looks like you've been through a lot," Po remarked.

Starlin nodded grimly, his hand unconsciously brushing the bandage at his side.

"We barely made it out of the Fifth Kingdom," he said. "The place we once called home is now unrecognizable."

Po wanted to ask why the kingdom was in such a state but held back out of politeness. Zap, ever the blunt one, didn't hesitate. "What happened?"

Starlin's eyes widened in surprise. "You haven't heard?" he asked. Then, with a sombre tone, he explained, "The kingdom to the East invaded us. We've been locked in a losing war ever since."

Evelyn sighed, her eyes distant. "For as long as I can remember, the Fifth and Sixth Kingdoms were like siblings," she began. "King Anthar of the Sixth was a kind man, a friend to our people."

She paused, recalling the memories. "He used to send help whenever we faced hard times. One year, a storm destroyed half of our harvest," she continued. "He sent wagons full of fruits and grains to keep our people fed through the winter. He'd always been someone we could count on."

Zap's ears perked up, curiosity filling his gaze. "That doesn't sound like someone who'd send an army to invade."

Evelyn's face darkened, and she glanced down at Anrar, who was listening intently, his small face etched with worry. She put a gentle hand on his head, as if to shield him from the uglier parts of the story.

"It wasn't like him," Evelyn murmured. "It all changed so suddenly. He went from a compassionate king to... a ghost. No one sees him now. They say he locks himself in his chamber, refusing visitors—even his closest advisors. And then... he sent his armies to claim our land, ordering them to kill anyone who resisted."

The wind howled around them, and the waves crashed against the shore with renewed fury, as if echoing the sorrow in Evelyn's voice. Zap flinched, casting a wary glance at the darkening horizon as if he could see the armies marching beyond.

Po's heart grew heavy as he listened. He'd seen kingdoms hurt by darkness and greed, but the betrayal of a friend was a unique wound. This wasn't just a war—it was a betrayal that shattered trust. He couldn't imagine what it must have felt like for the people of the Fifth Kingdom to be attacked by those they had trusted.

Starlin's jaw clenched, his gaze hardening. "I served as a guard in our capital. I watched friends fall to the Sixth Kingdom's soldiers, people I'd trained with, fought alongside. And all under the command of a king we'd once considered a friend."

Po swallowed, trying to process the weight of their words. "But... do you know why? Why would King Anthar do this?"

Evelyn shook her head, her face etched with sorrow and confusion. "No one knows. It's as if he became a different person overnight. But whatever the reason, it's our people who suffer."

Zap, who had been silent for a rare moment, finally spoke up, his voice uncharacteristically quiet. "That's terrible... and it sounds like he really cared about you all before. If he could do something like that, then... maybe it's not entirely his choice." His voice wavered, and Po noticed the uncharacteristic worry in his eyes.

Starlin's gaze softened as he looked at Zap. "I'd like to think that. But he's still the one giving the orders. And those orders have taken lives."

Anrar, who had been listening quietly, looked up at his mother with wide, fearful eyes. "Mama... will we ever go home again?"

Evelyn's face softened, and she pulled her son close, kissing the top of his head. "I don't know, sweet one. But wherever we are, as long as we're together, we'll be home." She glanced at Po and Zap, her eyes shining with quiet resolve. "It's not a place that keeps us safe, but the people we love."

Po felt a wave of sadness and admiration wash over him. Despite the darkness that had shattered their lives, Evelyn and Starlin clung to hope—something fragile, yet unbreakable. They had found strength in each other, in family and friendships that went beyond blood.

Po broke the silence, his voice gentle. "We're... trying to help, too. We've lost people, and I know it's different, but... I can't stand the thought of more lives lost to the darkness."

The wind and clouds began to subside, revealing a soft orange glow over the camp.

Starlin stood next to Po and placed a hand on his shoulder. "You can use our boat. We won't be returning home for quite a while." His voice was steady, but his gaze lingered on the horizon as if he could see the memories of his fallen comrades etched there.

They both gazed at the vast horizon stretching across the sea. "There's a sanctuary deep within the forest. Find it and tell the woman there that we sent you. You'll be safe," Po instructed, handing Starlin their weathered map.

As they prepared to leave, Anrar took Po's hand, pressing a small green crayon into his palm. "Take this," he said. "It's my favourite colour. Wherever you go, may it remind you are not alone."

Po closed his fingers around the crayon. He felt a strange warmth from it, as if it carried a fragment of Anrar's spirit, something innocent and pure. He looked at Anrar, gratitude shining in his eyes. "Thank you." He then turned to Evelyn and Starlin. "And thank you... for sharing your story, for trusting us."

With a final nod to Starlin, who clasped his hand firmly, and to young Anrar, who clung to his mother's side, Po and Zap turned toward the shore. The journey ahead was daunting, but they felt lighter for the stories shared, their purpose somehow clearer.

As they reached the edge of the Four Winds Coast, the waves crashing and roaring against the rocks, Po looked back once more, seeing the small, resilient family huddled around their fire. He could feel their hope, fragile but unyielding, carrying him forward.

Zap nudged him. "Ready?"

Po nodded, his hand tightening around the small green crayon. "Let's go."

Together, they pushed the small fishing boat from the shore and climbed aboard, the old wood creaking beneath them as they settled in. The boat rocked beneath the waves, and for a moment, Po had to steady himself, gripping the edge to keep his balance. The wind picked up with renewed force, sending sprays of icy seawater up and over the boat, leaving them damp and chilled. Salt stung Po's lips, and the cold seeped through his clothes. Yet, their sights remained firmly set on the horizon, the looming silhouette of the Fifth Kingdom just barely visible through the gray mist.

The waves soon grew fiercer, tossing the small boat like a leaf in a storm. Each swell felt like a mountain rising under them, only to crash down with enough force to make the entire vessel shudder. The boat swayed sharply, nearly pitching them overboard with each jarring drop. Po gritted his teeth, gripping the edge as his knuckles turned white. Beside him, Zap clung to the side, his ears flattened against the roar of the wind.

They both adjusted their grip, their resolve hardening as they pushed through each wave, determined to make it to the other side.

And though the waters churned violently, they held on.

15

XV. At Sea

The storm began to settle, but the journey still tested Po and Zap's endurance. Waves slapped at the boat, rain drizzled in cold, needling drops, and the mist clung low over the water, dulling their sense of direction. Exhausted but resolute, they rowed through the fading swells, each pull of the oars seeming to bring them deeper into the unknown.

The mist parted briefly, and a faint humming drifted over the waves. Po squinted, his hands frozen on the oars, as a familiar figure emerged through the gloom—a small boat, bobbing with an ease that seemed unaffected by the storm's lingering wrath. Po's eyes widened.

"Is that...?" he murmured, hardly daring to believe it.

Indeed, it was the travelling merchant, rowing toward them with the same casual, unbothered air he always seemed to have, his lips pursed in a tuneless hum. As he drew closer, his boat slowed, and he tipped his hat with a confident smile.

"Well, well," he called out over the water. "Look who's taken to the sea. Quite the adventurers you two have become! Seems no part of the kingdom is safe from your travels, eh?" His eyes sparkled with mischief, as if he held secrets he'd never share.

Po and Zap exchanged glances, a mixture of confusion and surprise on their faces.

"How...how did you find us?" Po asked, a bit warily.

"Oh, news travels fast, you know," the merchant said, his voice light as he resumed rowing alongside them. His tone then shifted as he leaned forward on his oars. "These aren't ordinary times, my friends, and the kingdoms are not what they once were." He paused, casting a meaningful look at the misty horizon. "Remember, when tides rise, it's not always the strongest who survive."

With that, he resumed his quiet humming, gave them a final tip of his hat, and rowed off into the mist, leaving Po and Zap staring after him, both unnerved and more curious than ever.

Zap huffed, scratching his ear as he watched the merchant's silhouette vanish. "That guy... he always leaves us with more questions than answers."

Po nodded, his brows drawn together in thought. "Yeah... but he's got me wondering. What exactly are we heading into?"

They fell into silence again. The mist thickened, casting an eerie gray hue over the sea. Hours passed in steady rowing, each pull of the oars making their arms ache, each swell seeming to drag them back.

After a while, Po broke the silence with a long sigh. "You know, Zap, everything we've been through... It kind of makes the problems back home seem..."

"...insignificant?" Zap finished, cutting him off.

Po nodded, feeling a warmth from their connection. "Yeah."

Zap perked up, striking a grin at Po. "You know what's weird?"

Before Po could respond, Zap continued. "At night, the fireflies always look like they're spelling out something, but I can never quite read it."

Po chuckled, quickly followed by Zap's laugh. "What are you talking about?"

The laugh seemed to lighten their spirits, and for a moment, the grimness of their journey faded into the background. But the calm was short-lived. A sudden, sharp chill swept over them, cutting through their clothes and chilling them to the bone. The clouds above thickened, darkening as if in anticipation of something ominous. The waves grew restless, rocking the boat harder with each passing swell.

Then they heard it—a low, guttural roar, echoing over the water like thunder.

Po's heart seized as he looked up, scanning the sky. Through the rolling clouds, a shadow appeared—a massive form with wings outstretched, casting a dark silhouette over the water. It was a dragon, its scales almost black, gleaming faintly with an unnatural, menacing light. Recognition sent a jolt of fear through Po; it was the same dragon they'd encountered back in Amberstone Ascent. However, something about it had changed. Its scales had darkened like ash, and its eyes glowed with an eerie intensity that hadn't been there before.

"Zap," Po whispered, his voice trembling, "that's... that's the same dragon from before. But it looks... different."

Zap's ears flattened against his head, and he instinctively crouched lower in the boat. "Why is it here? And... wait, Po... there's someone on its back."

Po squinted, his heart pounding as he spotted a figure astride the dragon. Cloaked in black robes that billowed in the wind, the figure held themselves with a dark, regal poise. The robes seemed to merge with the shadows around them, making it impossible to tell where the fabric ended, and the darkness began.

The dragon circled above, its enormous wings beating in slow, deliberate movements as it eyed the small boat below. Po and Zap stayed perfectly still, their breaths shallow, too terrified to make even the smallest sound. They were utterly exposed, a tiny, vulnerable speck in the vast expanse of the ocean.

For a moment, Po thought the rider had spotted them, his heart racing as the dragon banked lower. But then the figure seemed to shift their focus, directing the dragon's gaze toward something far off in the distance.

"Are... are they leaving?" Zap whispered, his voice barely audible.

The dragon gave one last bone-rattling roar, sending a wave of fear surging through Po and Zap. Then, with a powerful beat of its wings, it rose higher, the rider steering it northward, away from their boat. They watched in stunned silence as the dragon's silhouette shrank, disappearing into the dark clouds that hung over the distant horizon.

When the creature was finally gone, Zap let out a breath he'd been holding, slumping against the side of the boat. "I can't believe... we're still alive."

Po nodded, his heart still racing. "Me neither. But... that dragon, and whoever that was riding it..." He shook his head, struggling to process what he'd seen. "It felt like they were after something."

Zap glanced at the sky, his expression a mix of awe and fear. "Whatever it is they're looking for, let's hope we're not close by when they find it."

A short while later, Zap spotted something heading towards them from the West. A towering ship appeared, slicing through the gray fog as if summoned by some hidden force. It's dark, polished wood and elegant sails glided over the water with eerie grace, a silent predator in a vast, open sea.

Po gripped the oars and leaned forward, trying to make out the details of the ship. Its hull was ancient, crafted of darkened wood that shimmered with a faint metallic sheen. Intricate carvings of strange, twisting creatures and runes adorned its bow, symbols that seemed to twist under the mist as though alive.

"Po," Zap muttered, with determination in his voice, "Should we ask them for directions? We've been rowing for —"

Before he could finish, the ship slowed, drifting beside them. Po glanced up as a crewman leaned over the side, his piercing gray eyes watching them with an unsettling intensity. He was tall, with a thick gray beard that looked like it had weathered countless storms, and a crooked smile that did little to ease Po's suspicion.

"Lost, are you?" the man called, his voice carrying over the waves with a strange, almost musical quality.

Po hesitated but knew they couldn't turn back now. He raised his voice. "We're bound for the Fifth Kingdom. Just trying to reach safe shores."

The man let out a chuckle, his eyes gleaming with mirth that didn't quite reach his expression. "Heading for the Fifth Kingdom on that thing? You won't make it halfway, I'd wager."

He then gestured for them to come aboard, lowering a rope ladder into the water. "Safe shores, indeed. Well, why risk it alone? Come aboard. Captain's orders are to lend a hand to anyone on these waters. And, I'd say you two could use it."

Zap shot Po a wary glance, whispering, "Po, I don't know... this doesn't feel right."

Po's own apprehension flared, but he forced himself to shake it off. "We're out of options, Zap. They're offering help, and if we're going to make it, we'll need all the help we can get."

With a final nod, they climbed out of their boat and paddled closer. As they climbed up the rope ladder, Po felt an odd chill, like a shadow passing over his heart. The deck was spotless, gleaming under the dim light as though it had been meticulously polished. But the strangest part was the quietness—the only sound was the soft lapping of waves against the hull.

The crew moved with fluid precision, not a single wasted motion or word exchanged among them. Dressed in plain, well-worn clothes, they seemed more like townsfolk than sailors. But their eyes, all fixed on Po and Zap, held a strange, hungry gleam.

"Welcome aboard," said the gray-bearded man, extending a hand. His grip was cold as stone, his fingers surprisingly strong. "Name's Boryll. The captain'll want a word, I'm sure."

Po nodded and glanced around as he and Zap were led forward. The crew parted for them with eerie silence, each pair of eyes watching as they passed. An older woman with worn, calloused hands was coiling a rope, her gaze fixed and unblinking as Po passed. A young boy swept the deck with mechanical precision, his eyes glazed over, staring through them rather than at them.

They were led to the main cabin doors, and Po took a breath, preparing himself as Boryll knocked.

"Captain, we've guests aboard," he called, his voice ringing clear in the stillness.

The doors swung open, and they were ushered inside. The cabin was richly furnished but dim, lit only by flickering lanterns casting long shadows over the dark wood. Heavy curtains covered the windows, allowing only faint slivers of light to filter through. In the shadows at the far end, someone was sitting behind a massive, carved desk, their face obscured by darkness.

"Welcome," the figure said, voice smooth as silk. The figure rose, and Po's stomach lurched as he finally recognized the man.

Tezcat stepped forward, the familiar glint in his cold, calculating eyes sending a chill through Po's spine. He was dressed in his usual black armour, glinting faintly in the dim light. The crew fell silent, their heads lowered in reverence, like loyal subjects before a king.

Po swallowed hard, his fists clenched. "What do you want, Tezcat? You've already taken everything. What more could you possibly need?"

"Everything?" Tezcat echoed, feigning mild surprise. He began to circle them, his steps light and feline. "Not quite, Po. I've claimed the Fourth Kingdom, yes—but that's only the beginning. There are six kingdoms to bring under my and Epial's rule. And once they are... we will wield the power to reshape this world into a new age."

Po held his ground, his defiance sparking despite the odds. "You'll never control us. We'll fight until the end."

Tezcat's eyes narrowed, and he stopped, looking at Po with a faint trace of amusement. "Fight until the end, you say? How noble. How brave." His voice dropped to a menacing whisper, each word laced with barely concealed disdain. "But bravery alone won't save you from the storm I'm about to unleash."

Zap's tail twitched, his eyes fixed on Tezcat with a mixture of anger and fear. "So, what now? Gonna throw us overboard?"

Tezcat laughed softly, a dark, chilling sound that sent shivers down their spines. "Oh no," he said, his smile widening. "That would be too merciful."

He turned away, sweeping his gaze over the silent crew. "Prepare for battle," he commanded, his voice echoing through the cabin. The crew, as if woken from a trance, moved with sudden purpose, their steps synchronized and eerily swift.

Tezcat stepped closer to Po, his gaze cold and unyielding. "I'll let you fight, Po, since you're so determined to be brave. But I can assure you... this time, your courage will be your undoing."

The crew around them took their positions, their eyes now sharp, focused, and unwaveringly loyal to Tezcat. Weapons appeared in their hands as if conjured from thin air, each blade gleaming with an unnatural, ghostly light.

Po and Zap backed toward the door, instincts screaming to escape, but Tezcat raised a hand, and the door slammed shut, trapping them.

"Welcome to the end, Po," he whispered, his eyes glinting with cruel satisfaction. "Let's see how much bravery you truly have."

16

XVI. Wrath of the Deep

The flickering lanterns cast elongated shadows across the rich wood walls, painting Tezcat's smile into something sinister and distorted as he eyed them, a predator sizing up his prey. His cold gaze met Po's, and the corners of his mouth curled in a faint smirk.

Zap growled, his stance low and tense, while Po tightened his grip on his sword, willing his hands to steady. Despite the many encounters they'd survived, something about Tezcat's calculating calm, the ease with which he looked down on them, made him feel small.

"It's over, Tezcat," Po managed, his voice stronger than he felt. "Light will always win."

"Light?" Tezcat's smirk deepened, his voice almost pitying. "Such faith in something so fragile. Light flickers and fades at the slightest shadow, Po. Darkness endures. I endure. But your little quest?" He extended his hand, dark energy coiling around his fingers like smoke. "That ends here."

Without warning, Tezcat struck. A blast of dark energy tore across the small room, colliding with Po's hastily raised shield and sending him skidding back. Zap darted forward, baring his teeth, and lunged, only to have Tezcat sidestep him with ease, flicking a wrist and sending a dark ripple that knocked Zap against the wall.

"Is that all you've got?" Tezcat sneered, striding forward, each step echoing ominously on the floorboards. "You've fought shadows, yes, but not true darkness. You and your pet don't stand a chance."

Po gritted his teeth, rising to his feet. "We've faced monsters—creatures that would've crushed anyone else." His eyes hardened. "And we're still here."

Tezcat's laughter was low and mocking. "You still think you will win, don't you?" He raised a hand, magic swirling. "Let's stop pretending."

With a swift motion, he hurled another wave of darkness, a seething, inky force that split the air with a hiss. Po barely blocked it, the impact jarring him to the bone. The room itself seemed to tremble under the weight of Tezcat's power. The walls shuddered, lanterns swinging wildly, casting frantic shadows.

Zap gave Po a quick glance, and Po caught the unspoken message in his eyes. They couldn't overpower Tezcat in here. Not trapped in the narrow confines of this cabin. Po gave a slight nod, signalling his understanding.

He dove to the left, forcing Tezcat's attention in that direction while Zap darted right, scrambling toward the door. With a fierce swipe of his claws, Zap shattered the latch, and the door burst open, slamming against the wall.

They stumbled out onto the deck, gasping in the sudden rush of cold, rain-laden wind. The storm had intensified, sheets of rain lashing the ship, waves as tall as houses crashing against the hull. Lightning split the sky, illuminating the deck for a brief moment. The ship lurched underfoot, nearly throwing Po and Zap to the slick planks, and they scrambled for balance, Tezcat striding after them.

Tezcat emerged from the cabin with an unsettling calm, untouched by the chaos. His presence, dark and resolute, seemed to cut through the storm itself. He raised one hand, and a wave of shadow pulsed outward, knocking back crew members like ragdolls as they fought to stay upright.

"Did you really think you could just run away?" Tezcat's voice rang out, unnaturally amplified against the roar of the sea. "Your resistance is nothing more than a delay of your death." He extended his arms, and the shadows around him thickened, reaching out with sinister intent.

Po gritted his teeth, pulling Zap to his feet. "Zap, we need to distract him."

Zap nodded, his usual glint of humour absent. "Say less."

With that, Zap leapt forward, dodging between the pulses of darkness with a surprising agility, snapping and darting close to Tezcat to keep his attention split. Po circled around, sword in hand, and struck from behind. Tezcat turned just in time to parry with a twist of his wrist, deflecting Po's blow with a shock of energy that rattled his bones.

"Is that the best you can do, Po?" Tezcat sneered, pushing him back with a surge of force that sent Po sliding across the wet deck.

Before he could press the advantage, a guttural roar pierced the air, and the ship lurched violently. The three of them staggered as the ship's timbers groaned under the pressure. A massive tentacle, as thick as a tree trunk, slammed onto the deck with a thunderous crash, splintering the wood.

A colossal, ancient sea monster rose from the water, its eyes glowing a sickly green, tentacles writhing with terrible strength. The creature's gleaming eyes bore into Tezcat like molten emeralds.

It was filled with a rage as old as the ocean itself. It seemed less a monster and more an avenger, rising from the depths to punish those who dared to disrupt its domain. The sea answered its fury, waves crashing higher as if summoned by the beast's will.

One tentacle lashed out, nearly taking Tezcat with it. He dodged, for the first time showing a flicker of alarm.

Po seized the chance, running forward and slashing at the tentacle. His blade sank into the thick, rubbery flesh, but it only enraged the creature. The tentacle whipped around, knocking him off his feet and nearly tossing him overboard.

"Po!" Zap cried, grabbing his friend by the wrist and hauling him back just before another tentacle crashed down inches away.

Tezcat, regaining his composure, sneered at the beast, his hand lifting as if to control it—but nothing happened. The sea monster lashed out again, clearly beyond even Tezcat's dark influence.

"So, you're not as powerful as you thought," Po panted, his eyes fixed on Tezcat.

Tezcat's cold smile returned. "We'll see." He turned to his crew, his voice cutting through the storm. "Restrain them!"

The crew, who had until now stood still as if in a trance, snapped to attention. Swords gleamed in their hands, and they moved forward with single-minded precision, eyes locked on Po and Zap. There was no hesitation, no fear—only the icy obedience of soldiers under an unbreakable spell.

Po and Zap stood back-to-back, breathing heavily, surrounded. Po tightened his grip on his sword, meeting Zap's gaze with a nod.

"We're outnumbered," Zap whispered, "but I'm not going down without a fight."

"Nor am I," Po replied, and with a cry, they surged forward, throwing themselves into the fray.

Po met the first crewman head-on, parrying a brutal strike and countering with a swift cut that sent the man sprawling. Another lunged at him, but Po ducked under his swing, landing a solid blow to the man's midsection. Every clash of steel rang out in defiance, but for every opponent they felled, two more stepped forward to take their place.

Nearby, Zap darted and weaved through the legs of the advancing soldiers, his claws and teeth flashing in the dim light as he snapped at ankles and tore at exposed hands. His small size made him difficult to catch, and he used it to his advantage, tripping one man who stumbled backward, only to be struck down by Po's blade.

But the odds were against them. Tezcat watched with cruel amusement, his gaze shifting occasionally to the thrashing sea monster as if calculating his next move. Lightning cracked above, illuminating his face—a mask of satisfaction, as if he revelled in the storm, his power magnified by the chaos around him.

Suddenly, a massive tentacle came down across the deck, sweeping away soldiers and crew alike in a brutal swing. It slammed into the mast, cracking the thick wood, and sent a splintered beam crashing down between Po and Zap, dividing them.

"Zap!" Po shouted, panic lacing his voice as the debris cut off his line of sight.

"Still here!" Zap called back, though his voice was faint over the roar of the storm and the monstrous creature's enraged cries.

The ship bucked wildly, tossing Po against the railing. His head throbbed, his vision swimming as he struggled to regain his footing. A shadow loomed over him, and he looked up just in time to see Tezcat approaching, a wicked gleam in his eyes.

"This is the end for you, Po," Tezcat said softly, his voice like a dagger's edge. "Did you really think you could challenge me? You're just a boy with a toy sword."

Po forced himself to stand, every muscle screaming in protest. He met Tezcat's gaze, fire blazing in his eyes. "I may be just a boy," he spat, "but I wield the power of light, and light dispels all shadows."

He lunged forward, swinging his sword with every ounce of strength he had left. Tezcat blocked the blow with a sneer, twisting his wrist and sending Po's blade clattering across the deck. Before Po could react, Tezcat struck, knocking him down with a blast of dark energy that sent a wave of pain searing through him.

Po crumpled to the deck, gasping for air, his vision blurring. But as he lay there, struggling to move, he felt a small, familiar shape press against his side.

Zap. Despite everything, his friend was still by his side.

"Get up, Po," Zap said, his voice a fierce whisper. "We're not done yet."

With Zap's support, Po managed to stagger to his feet, his gaze locking onto Tezcat's with renewed defiance. "You may have power, Tezcat, but you'll never understand why we fight. And that's why you'll lose."

Tezcat's eyes narrowed, and he raised his hand, shadows gathering around him in a swirling vortex. But before he could strike, the sea monster's tentacle smashed onto the deck once more, slamming directly between them. The ship bucked under the impact, throwing all three of them back.

A surge of water flooded the deck, cold and biting, as the sea monster's fury reached a fever pitch. Its tentacles coiled around the ship, squeezing with enough force to make the wooden hull groan and splinter. Lightning flashed, illuminating its monstrous form as it loomed over the ship like an avenging deity.

The deck tilted, and Po and Zap found themselves sliding toward the edge, the churning sea waiting below. Po grabbed hold of a rope, clinging to it with white-knuckled desperation as Zap clung to his side.

Tezcat rose to his feet on the other side of the deck, his expression a mask of rage. "This ends now!" he shouted, his voice a thunderous command that seemed to cut through the storm.

Po's grip slipped, his strength waning as the ship continued to tilt. But as he looked up, he saw a glimmer of hope—a crack forming in the ship's hull where one of the sea monster's tentacles had struck. Water was flooding in, weakening the vessel with each passing second.

"Zap!" Po gasped, his voice hoarse. "The ship—it's breaking apart!"

Zap's eyes widened as he looked around, realization dawning. "We've got to get off this thing!"

But Tezcat was advancing again, his focus narrowing on Po with deadly intent. "You think you can escape me?" he sneered, his voice carrying an edge of madness. "I am the shadows. I am darkness incarnate. I am—"

He was cut off as the ship gave a final, shuddering lurch, the sea monster's tentacles tearing through the weakened hull with a sickening crack. The vessel split in two, and Po and Zap were thrown forward, tumbling toward the edge of the deck as the ship began to sink.

Po's last memory was of cold water closing over his head, the roar of the storm fading into silence.

Just before the darkness claimed him, Po thought he saw a figure—faint and shimmering, like an apparition—standing on the edge of the wreckage. Linfer. Her golden eyes were calm, filled with the same fierce determination he'd seen in their last moments together. She looked at him, her expression soft but resolute, as if urging him onward, to keep fighting.

And then, with one final look of encouragement, she faded into the mist and the churning sea, leaving him with a strange, unshakable sense of peace.

Then, everything went dark.

17

❧

XVII. The Bitter End

Po felt himself drifting, weightless, as if cradled by some soft, unseen force. He floated through a realm of light and warmth, wrapped in a sensation so gentle it was as though he'd returned to the comfort of his childhood. Sunlight filtered down in soft, golden beams that felt familiar, like something he hadn't experienced in years. A winding path appeared beneath him, bordered by beds of moss and wildflowers that glowed with colours too vibrant to exist in reality.

For a moment, he stood still, confusion mixing with a calm he couldn't explain. The peace felt tangible, like a memory come to life. *Where am I?* he wondered. But the peace he felt seemed real, tangible. His feet found their way onto the path, each step muffled by the springy moss beneath him. The air was warm, carrying a faint scent of honey and dew, so comforting that it made Po's heart ache with a homesickness he couldn't quite place.

The sound of soft footsteps caught his attention. Po turned to see a small, familiar creature—a tufted, purple-furred animal with wide, inquisitive eyes. It was the same creature he and Zap had followed once before, though he couldn't recall where or when. Its eyes met his, gentle and inviting, as if it recognized him. Without thinking, Po followed it, feeling inexplicably drawn forward, his steps quickening as he trailed the small creature down the winding path.

As they walked, he noticed symbols flickering in the air, faint and ethereal—images of places he'd seen, faces he'd known. They seemed to hover just out of reach, vanishing when he tried to focus on them. A gentle breeze stirred around him, and he heard whispers in its wake—whispers that called his name, each murmur like a familiar voice he couldn't quite remember.

The creature bounded forward, stopping occasionally to look back at him with bright, understanding eyes, as if urging him onward. He followed, his steps quickening until the path opened into a clearing. Po froze, his breath catching in his throat.

Towering before him was a tree so magnificent it seemed almost otherworldly. Its roots sprawled outward, sinking deep into the earth, each gnarled twist alive with ancient power. The branches arched high into the sky, draped with golden orbs that floated like lanterns in a soft, rhythmic sway. Birds with shimmering feathers flitted through its branches, their soft chirps filling the air with a music that resonated deep within him. Small, gentle creatures with luminous eyes darted around its roots, playing in the light and casting playful shadows over the moss-covered ground.

Po stared, awe-struck. *This... this feels sacred*, he thought, an overwhelming sense of reverence washing over him. The tree felt alive in a way that transcended anything he'd ever known, radiating a warmth that made his heart feel both fragile and indestructible. "It's beautiful..." he murmured, stepping closer, feeling as if the tree was pulling him in.

But as he moved forward, something changed. The warmth in the air cooled, the light around the tree dimming as if some shadow had crossed over it. Po paused, a shiver prickling at his spine. The golden orbs hanging from the branches faded, shifting from soft gold to a sickly, tarnished green. One by one, they flickered, their glow waning, before darkening entirely, like candles snuffed out by an unseen hand.

Po's breath quickened. The once vibrant leaves above him began to wither, curling inward and falling, brittle and lifeless, to the ground. He looked around, watching as the bright birds took flight, their chirps silenced as they vanished into the encroaching shadows. The creatures at the roots scurried away, disappearing into burrows as cracks spread through the earth around the tree.

"What... what's happening?" he whispered, fear coiling in his stomach. He took a step back, but his gaze remained fixed on the tree as its bark darkened, the once-lustrous wood splitting and cracking, transforming into something twisted and hollow. The branches, once spread wide and welcoming, now looked skeletal, stretching out like claws against the darkening sky.

The air grew colder, the warmth that had once comforted him replaced by a biting chill that seeped into his bones. He could feel an oppressive darkness settling over him, as though the tree itself was sapping the light from his soul.

And then he heard it—a guttural, echoing roar that reverberated through the air, shaking the ground beneath him. Po's heart pounded, his skin prickling as he looked up into the darkening sky. There, soaring through the clouds, was the massive, ominous form of the dragon.

Its scales were nearly black, gleaming with an unnatural, sickly sheen that made it appear as though it had been born of the shadows themselves. Its wings beat against the air, each stroke sending ripples of darkness across the landscape. And atop the dragon's back sat a figure cloaked in flowing black robes, their face obscured by shadows that seemed to cling to them like a second skin.

Po felt his stomach churn with dread. The dragon rider, he thought, a cold terror seizing him as he recalled the figure he had seen only recently over the waves. The rider's presence felt like an insidious force, a malevolent weight that pressed down on the air around him.

The dragon let out another deafening roar, circling above the tree as its rider raised an arm, pointing downward. Dark clouds churned above them, thickening until the tree itself seemed swallowed in a sinister haze. Po watched as the remaining leaves on the tree blackened and fell, swirling through the air like ashes.

"No... this can't be happening..." he whispered, stumbling backward as the tree continued to wither. The ground beneath him quaked, fractures forming in the earth as if it, too, were breaking under the weight of this darkness.

The rider and the dragon circled lower, each pass sending a wave of dread through Po's chest. He could barely breathe, his body frozen in terror, his legs unwilling to move. He wanted to look away, to turn and run, but the sight of the dragon descending upon the dying tree held him captive.

Suddenly, a sharp crack split the air, and Po saw the tree's roots begin to tear apart, twisting like tortured limbs reaching toward him. The once-mighty tree, now reduced to a desolate, skeletal husk, seemed to turn its focus to Po. The branches, once soft and sheltering, now loomed over him like claws ready to strike.

Po stumbled back, tripping over a root as he struggled to escape. "No! Get away!" he gasped, feeling the shadows closing in around him, pulling him deeper into their grasp. The dragon circled even lower, its eyes blazing as it locked onto Po, as though sensing his fear and relishing in it.

And then, in one swift, fluid motion, the rider extended a gloved hand toward Po. The air grew cold as ice, a force as unyielding as iron gripping him, holding him in place. The dragon's roar filled his ears, drowning out every other sound, its piercing gaze fixed on him with a hunger that terrified him to his core.

Just as Po felt himself slipping, falling into the abyss that seemed to stretch beneath him, the entire scene fractured, splintering like shattered glass. The tree, the dragon, the figure—all of it broke apart, spinning away into darkness.

Po fell backward, plunging into an empty void as the remnants of the vision faded around him. The last thing he saw was the skeletal tree reaching out to him, its branches stretching like dark, twisted fingers, seeming to follow him even into the depths of the void.

And then, silence.

*

As Po's eyes fluttered open, the dream's darkness faded, replaced by a hazy, smoke-filled sky. The warmth and light of the dream clung to him, but it faded like morning mist, leaving only the cold, sharp edges of reality. His body ached from head to toe, bruises and cuts throbbing with a dull pain that reminded him of the recent fight. He lay still for a moment, his chest heaving as he tried to process what was real and what wasn't, the nightmare clinging to him like a second skin. But the smell of salt, smoke, and charred wood quickly reminded him where he was.

Slowly, he pushed himself up on shaking arms, feeling the sand shifting beneath him. He was on a desolate shore, rough grains of sand sticking to his hands and the wetness of his clothing. Just beyond him, the waves crashed over what was left of the ship—a ruin of splintered wood and broken masts scattered across the coastline. Barrels and crates bobbed in the shallow water, some drifting farther out to sea, others barely recognizable under the thick black smoke curling into the sky.

The ship... The memory of the battle surged back, and panic seized him. He whipped his head around, scanning his surroundings frantically.

"Zap?" he croaked, his throat dry and raw. He staggered to his feet, squinting against the smoke as he searched the water and the debris-strewn beach for any sign of his friend. His heartbeat thundered in his ears as he took in the scene around him.

Wreckage littered the water, pieces of wood, torn sails, barrels, and loose planks drifting in the surf like a grim reminder of the storm they'd faced. Amid the flotsam, several bodies floated listlessly, faces pale, their limbs slack and lifeless. Po's breath hitched at the sight, and he forced himself to look away, bile rising in his throat.

"Zap!" His voice cracked as he called again, desperation clawing at him as he moved along the shore, scanning the scattered wreckage and hoping for a glimpse of Zap's familiar, furred form. His gaze swept over the beach, and despair welled up in his chest. He opened his mouth to call again, but his voice caught, faltering into silence. "Please... not you, too," he whispered, the words almost lost to the crashing waves.

And then, as he stumbled over a piece of driftwood, his gaze fell upon something farther down the shore. Po froze, his blood running cold. There, impaled on a jagged shard of wood protruding from the sand, was Tezcat.

The Shadow Twin lay with his face turned toward the sky, eyes wide and unseeing, his body twisted at an unnatural angle. Blood trickled from the wound in his chest, darkening the sand beneath him. The once-feared figure, the one who had haunted Po's steps, who had taken so many lives and spread darkness across the kingdoms, was now motionless—a lifeless, broken shell.

Po's heart twisted as he took in the sight. For so long, Tezcat had been the dark figure looming over him, the villain who seemed untouchable, undefeatable. And now, here he was, his ambition extinguished, his malevolent power snuffed out. Po felt a wave of conflicting emotions flood through him—relief, disbelief, and a strange, hollow emptiness.

It's over, he thought, a shiver running down his spine. *He's... gone.*

But the victory felt incomplete. The weight of Tezcat's death didn't bring the sense of triumph he'd imagined. It was empty, tinged with bitterness, for in this moment of finality, he realized that he had lost something far more precious.

"Zap..." he whispered, his voice trembling. The absence of his friend felt like a wound, raw and agonizing, cutting deeper than any enemy blade ever could. The joy he should have felt at Tezcat's death, the relief of a battle finally won, was swallowed by a sinking despair. He'd faced everything with Zap at his side, his unwavering companion, his source of strength. And now, on this desolate shore, Po was alone.

The silence stretched around him, broken only by the soft lapping of the waves and the crackling of fires from the wreckage. He sank to his knees, his fingers digging into the sand as he stared at Tezcat's lifeless body, the reality settling heavily over him. The threat had been vanquished, yes—but at what cost?

A sharp ache formed in his chest, a deep, unyielding sorrow that left him feeling smaller, more vulnerable than he'd ever felt.

He had faced darkness, he had fought with everything he had, but now, without Zap, the world felt colder, less certain.

"Zap..." he whispered again, his voice barely a breath.

And as he knelt there, surrounded by the wreckage of both ship and soul, a single ray of sunlight pierced through the clouds, falling upon him like a distant promise. Po closed his eyes, a single tear slipping down his cheek as the wind carried the lingering echoes of the battle they had fought, and the memories of the friend he had yet to find.

Po lifted his head, feeling the weight of the promise he was making. If Zap was alive, he would find him.

No matter what.